Praise for The David Brand[stetter...]

"I can only applaud the republicati[on...] Dave Brandstetter books. I've increasingly come to regard the phrase '*an important writer of crime fiction*' as oxymoronic, but if one's going to use the label, Hansen's not an unreasonable bearer of it."

—Lawrence Block

"Incredible books, much overlooked."

—Jeff Abbott

"The Brandstetter books are classics of the private eye genre ... It's great to see them available again."

—Peter Robinson

"First published over fifty years ago now, Hansen's novels are not just clever and compelling stories, but to my mind they are also a feat of incredible bravery. I wish I'd discovered him sooner."

—Russ Thomas, CrimeReads

"Hansen is one of the best we have ... [He] knows how to tell a tough, unsentimental, fast-moving story in an exceptionally urbane literary style."

—*New York Times Book Review*

"After forty years, Hammett has a worthy successor."

—*The Times* (London)

"Mr. Hansen is an excellent craftsman, a compelling writer."

—*The New Yorker*

"Apart from its virtues as fiction, Hansen's *Early Graves* is a field correspondent's breathtaking dispatch from a community in the midst of disaster."

—*Time*

A COUNTRY OF OLD MEN

THE DAVE BRANDSTETTER NOVELS

Fadeout (1970)
Death Claims (1973)
Troublemaker (1975)
The Man Everybody Was Afraid Of (1978)
Skinflick (1979)
Gravedigger (1982)
Nightwork (1984)
The Little Dog Laughed (1986)
Early Graves (1987)
Obedience (1988)
The Boy Who Was Buried This Morning (1990)
A Country of Old Men (1991)

A COUNTRY
OF OLD MEN

JOSEPH HANSEN

A DAVE BRANDSTETTER NOVEL

SYNDICATE BOOKS
NEW YORK

First published in 1991
by Viking

This edition published in 2023
by Syndicate Books
www.syndicatebooks.com

Distributed by
Soho Press, Inc.
227 W 17th Street
New York, NY 10011

ISBN 978-1-68199-069-9
eISBN 978-1-68199-080-4

Printed in the United States of America

10 9 8 7 6 5 4 3 2 1

To Dave Brandstetter's friends around the world:
Hail and farewell!

1

The MAN AT *the door had a white moustache and goatee. His tweed jacket looked new, but it wouldn't button over his big belly. He wore a red-striped cotton shirt, new blue denims, crepe-soled shoes, and one of those shapeless canvas hats sold in drugstores, cheap, so that if you lost it on a trip you wouldn't mind too much. Dave didn't know him.*

"Do something for you?" he said.

"It's Helmers." The voice was a rumbling bass. He held out a thick, liver-spotted hand. "Been that long, has it?"

Dave shook the hand, amazed. The man had changed beyond recognition. "Jack," he said. "Come in." He stepped back, motioning at the long, raftered room.

Helmers came in, heavy, slow, an old bear, his breathing audible. "Twenty years, I guess." Dave let the door stand open. Though it wasn't yet noon, and the place was shaded by big, untrimmed trees, it had gathered heat. The windows and the skylight over the sleeping loft stood open, but there was a faint smell of horse—the place had once been a stable. "Let me take that jacket." Helmers let him take it. Dave carried it and the hat down the room to a hatrack and hung them up. He called, "Sit down. I'll bet you'd like a beer."

"You're on," Helmers said, and dropped with a sigh into a wing chair by the broad fireplace. "Sorry to come unannounced, but your telephone's always busy."

"Unplugged." Dave bent to take brown bottles of Dos Equis from the small refrigerator back of the bar. "I've retired, but the world doesn't want to accept that. And I get fed up with explaining." He brought back the dewy bottles and a pair of tall glasses, provided Helmers with one of each, and sat on the brick surround of the raised hearth. "How's Katherine these days?"

"Dead. Cancer. Four years now."

"My phone wasn't unplugged back then," Dave said.

"I didn't notify anybody. There wasn't any service. She and I were one person, Dave." That had been true, and the strongest reason Dave and Helmers saw little of each other once the writer had married. Katherine seemed all the human company he'd needed. Dave had visited them a couple of times. He'd seen why Helmers felt as he did. She was beautiful, intelligent, informed about a world of subjects. "When we parted I wanted it to be between the two of us. Nobody else—" He broke the sentence, left the thought, tilted the bottle and watched the dark beer pile up high foam in the glass. "I haven't come to bust up your retirement." Helmers pushed his glasses up on his nose. It was a habit he'd had even as a teenager. He and Dave had gone to high school together. His nose had never offered glasses much support. "Just for expert advice. There's been an unexplained death. No more real than the ones I think up for my books. But it annoys me. You see—it's mine."

"Exaggerated," Dave said. "Like Mark Twain's."

"I can't trace who started the rumor, but it's all over. Not just LA. New York, too. Connecticut—I teach in Connecticut sometimes in the summer. Vermont, Oregon, New Mexico. Anyplace people know me." He downed some of the beer, wiped his moustache and chin whiskers with a hand. Remembered. Set the glass aside, tilted his broad behind in the chair to dig a crushed envelope out of a hip pocket. He waved it at Dave. It was an airmail envelope with exotic stamps in the corner. "From Japan. This morning. Total stranger." He pulled a letter from the envelope, rattled it open. "They are saying you are dead. I do not believe it. I love your books, and do not want them to stop, so please write to me to prove it is not true." Helmers chuckled, shook his head, slid the letter into the envelope, stuffed it away in his hip pocket again. "Can you beat it? Why?"

Dave got to his feet, peered up at the tall bookshelves that flanked the fireplace and surrounded the windows along the wall. He took a few steps, reached up, came back with a dozen books that he stacked on the bricks at Helmers's elbow. He sat down again. Helmers blinked at the books, at him, picked up a book, opened it. Dave knew what he saw. His own big, sprawling handwriting. *To Dave Brandstetter, with best wishes from an old friend, Jack Helmers.* And a date. They kept landing up in the mailbox, in Jiffy bags, one a year, sometimes two. He read them and wrote a few words of admiration. That's how they kept in touch—the only way. Today that seemed a little sad. Helmers closed the book.

"You trying to tell me something?"

"A writer's autograph in a book is worth more when he's dead. Some collector couldn't make up his mind to shuck out a hundred dollars for a signed copy of your first novel, so the bookseller used the clincher—told him you'd died."

"And the collector told a friend, who told two friends?" Helmers laid the book back on the stack. "Ridiculous."

"You have a better explanation?" Dave said.

Helmers grunted and quaffed more beer. "Ah, that's the real thing," he said. "No—human nature being what it is, you're probably right." He emptied the rest of the beer from the bottle into the glass. "But I wish it would stop. I've been feeling mortal enough without it. Suddenly the book publishing business has changed—I've written that big novel I always wanted to, about turning eighteen in Pasadena, fifty years ago. Nobody will publish it." A sigh. "Kidney stones, bad back, high blood pressure—I'm falling apart."

"Welcome to the club."

"You look fine. Not an extra pound on you."

Dave grimaced. "Thin isn't everything." He watched Helmers light a cigarette. "When I quit those I thought I'd balloon, but I didn't."

"Maybe you don't eat enough," Helmers said.

"Join me for lunch," Dave said. "You'll see."

Helmers said, "Come to think of it, I read in the paper you'd bought a restaurant. Max Romano's. We ate there a few times, didn't we, forties, fifties? Nice place."

Dave looked at his watch. "We can go there now."

Helmers blinked. "God damn. That will make a change. You know—I haven't eaten in a restaurant in years. Nobody to go with—all dead. All I do is stay home and write."

"It's still a nice place," Dave said. "Come on."

For forty years and more it had been Dave's custom to enter Max Romano's through the steamy kitchen with its heady smells of garlic and cheese, basil and oregano, to throw a smiling salute to the dour, sunken-cheeked chef Alex Giacometti and to nod to and speak the names of the other kitchen help on his way through. He'd had to buy the restaurant to keep this privilege, when Max died last year and a nephew from New York had threatened to turn the place to tall clear glass walls, pale enamels, cane-seated chairs, sleek floors, and nouvelle cuisine. Dave couldn't let that happen. Max's place was more a part of his life history than any house he'd ever lived in. It was filled with memories and ghosts he couldn't let go. Money was no problem. His father had owned California's largest insurance company, Medallion Life, and when he died a few blondes back left Dave one third of the shares. He didn't even know how much money he had. He figured it would embarrass him to know. Alex had fretted— he was a chef, he'd never managed a business in his life, didn't know if he could. But he was doing fine.

Now Dave ushered Helmers through the steel-clad, round-windowed swing doors out of the kitchen heat and clatter into the shadowy cool of the restaurant itself. Most of the white-naperied, candle-lit tables were occupied. A cheerful hum of voices, jingle of ice in glasses, clicking of forks on china greeted them. Dave led Helmers across deep carpeting toward the quiet corner table Max had always reserved for him. Cecil Harris sat there. A tall, lanky young black who worked in television news as a field reporter and producer, Cecil lived with Dave. He looked worried now, and stood up before Dave and Helmers could sit down.

"Call Madge," he said. "She needs your help. Been trying to reach you all morning. So have I."

"Jack Helmers," Dave said. "Cecil Harris."

They shook hands. Helmers said, "Nice to know you."

"I enjoy your books," Cecil said.

"Sit down," Dave told them both. "I'll be right back."

When Dave returned from telephoning, Avram David was handing menus to Helmers and Cecil. Avram, who'd come here an immigrant kid from Israel and been a waiter at Max's for years, was now the maître d'. He'd never replace fat, jovial Max Romano, with his laughing affection for everybody who came in, but he brought large, luminous, long-lashed brown eyes to the job, and a slow smile that smoldered with sex. Now that Dave thought of it, the new streaks of gray in Avram's hair made him look startlingly like Omar Sharif.

"Mr. Brandstetter," he said, and pulled out Dave's chair for him. "The scallops came fresh this morning."

Dave sat down. "Then let it be the scallops. Glenlivet first, and a spinach salad, please." Dave saw that Cecil was drinking Perrier water with a slice of lime. He smelled what Helmers was drinking—sour mash whiskey. He could smell things sharply these days, now that he'd quit smoking. "Gentlemen?"

"Spinach salad sounds good to me." Helmers peered through his glasses, poked a thick finger at the menu. "Kidneys *a la moutarde*. My wife used to cook those."

Avram nodded. "We'll try to do as well." He raised dark eyebrows at Cecil. "Avocado stuffed with crab meat?"

"You got it. Mustn't get too full. Need a clear head. Big afternoon's work ahead of me."

Dave said, "You can't come with me to Madge's? I was hoping you'd drive."

"Sorry. Lot of cutting and splicing to do before five. Bad location sound. Have to dub narration on all of it. Write the copy." He read a big black sports watch on his wrist. "I don't know how I'm going to do it. What's up with Madge? All she'd tell me was she wanted you."

"Something about a lost child wandering on the beach. Who saw, or says he saw, a murder."

Cecil moaned. "Oh, no. Tell her to call the police."

"I told her, but she insists I talk to the boy first. He's very small, and it's a very wild story—when the murderer saw that he'd seen her, she kidnapped him. Madge says he appears to have been beaten." Dave wistfully watched Helmers light a cigarette, inhale, and blow the smoke away.

"Little kids lie all the time," Cecil said.

"Madge doesn't know anything about little kids." Dave sighed. "I don't relish driving all the way down there."

"Is this Madge Dunstan, the designer?" Helmers said. "Malibu—right? Haven't seen her in years. Matter of fact, it must have been with you. Right here."

Cecil said, "Dave, don't take another case. Please?"

The last one had been close to fatal—not just for him but for Cecil, too. Dave was getting too old to chase felons with sane hope of catching them. His reflexes were slowing down. His wits weren't as sharp as they once were. He'd set a trap last time he'd been sure would work. It hadn't worked. The wrong man had stepped into it in the dark, and Dave had been taken by surprise. That wouldn't have happened back when he was on his game. He smiled at Cecil. Not cheerfully, but meaning it. "I won't."

His Glenlivet arrived, a double in a wide, squat glass with ice. He tasted it, and started to reach across for the pack of Winstons beside Helmers's bread plate. But Cecil gave him a stern look, and he drew his hand back. The tang of the cigarette smoke was tormenting. What good was a drink without a cigarette? Health-mad antihedonists were ruining his life. Cecil wasn't one of those. He just wanted Dave to live a long time. Dave wasn't so sure that was worthwhile without vices. But he sighed now, rummaged a warm slice of fresh-baked bread from under a napkin in a basket, buttered it, and chewed it while he drank. He'd get used to making do sometime, he supposed, not really believing it.

The spinach salads arrived. Helmers attacked his. "I live in Topanga, you know," he said, mouth full. "It's on my way. I'll drive you, if you can get my car to me later."

"No problem." Dave's friend and mechanic Kevin Nakamura would do it. "We'll have to stop and buy some small-boy clothes. Madge says all he's wearing is a T-shirt and briefs, and they're filthy. As he is."

2

EUCALYPTUS, PINE OAKS, mountain holly had grown up around Helmers's place and hid it almost completely from the road. The writer swung the Jaguar into a rutted dirt driveway and halted it there with the engine running. Grunting with the effort, he got out of the car and stepped to a rural mailbox on which the red-painted name HELMERS had faded to a pink so faint it was hard to make out. The hinges of the mailbox door squeaked as he opened it. He pulled out a small carton and a few envelopes, shut the box, got stiffly back into the Jaguar again, and slammed the door. He patted the carton.

"My new book," he said.

They jounced on up the driveway to the house, unpainted cedar, with decks and tall windows. Dave recollected when it was new and how proud Helmers had been of it then. He'd started life a poor kid—really poor. His father had lost his grain business in the Depression, Midwest somewhere, the Dust Bowl. In Pasadena the man, already past sixty, had found it difficult to find work. A slim, handsome kid, Jack during high school had always had to earn money at this odd job and that. Dave, whose father even then had a Midas touch, had wondered how Jack stood it. But he was always cheerful, always optimistic. He was going to be the best writer America ever saw. It was only a matter of time.

It hadn't gotten quite that good. Twenty years of struggle lay ahead. But with Katherine always rooting for him, no matter how many novels and stories came winging back from New York rejected, he'd never stopped believing he'd make it some day. Dave liked Helmers, but as the years dragged on, it looked more and more certain to Dave that Helmers was one of life's losers.

Then, suddenly, what had been bundles of wastepaper to editors before became publishable. And by the time he was forty, Helmers was earning a living from his books—not much of a living, but enough so he didn't have to clerk in bookstores or type bills of lading in back offices at movie studios any longer. The books weren't the great American novels he'd dreamed of writing when he was editor of the high school paper, and used to chatter excitedly to Dave about the future. They were detective novels.

But they were literate, reviewers found something elegant about them, and slowly they built him a readership. Sometimes, when he sent Dave a new book, he'd enclose a note. He was published all over Europe now, and in Japan, and his publishers kept the books in print here in the States. He built this house—he'd called it the house that Kenniston built because Kenniston was the detective hero of his books—on money he'd earned writing, and he was proud of that. Which maybe meant that he, too, had sometimes, along with Dave and other friends, doubted he'd ever manage it.

But now, as Dave got out of the Jaguar to go around and get into the driver's seat, he saw that time and the weather and above all neglect had taken a toll on the house. The decks slumped. The windows were dusty and rain-streaked and hadn't been washed, it looked like, for years. Inside them, curtains hung torn and discolored by rain that had got to them because somebody'd forgotten to close the windows. The varnish on the front door had cracked and half of it peeled off. Cats slept in the speckled sunlight on the deck among neglected plants in pots. Dogs barked when Helmers put his key in the lock.

"I know murder's urgent business," he called, "but come in for just a minute, will you?" He pushed open the door, and a business card fluttered to the deck. Dave picked it up, handed it to him. Helmers grunted. "Goodman, again, real estate man. Told him I won't sell. Nice young fellow, thoughtful, helpful, but he won't take no for an answer." The house smelled of cats. The floor was stacked with dusty newspapers. Bookcases overflowed. Magazines, catalogs, books, videotapes, records filled the chairs and sofa, avalanches of unopened mail. On the walls, pictures hung crooked. Spiderwebs connected handsome but dusty hand-thrown pots on the mantelpiece. The empty trays of TV dinners made a crooked stack on the television set. Dogs came through the clutter, tongues hanging, tails wagging—small brown dogs of no certain breed but cheerful, sniffing Dave's pant legs, jumping up at Helmers, who patted them and spoke their names and told them to behave themselves.

"They never see strangers," he said.

Katherine would have been more than upset to see the place. She'd have wept. She kept it spotless, glowing. Dave remembered that. She wasn't any Craig's wife. It was a house that put the visitor at ease. Casual. Comfortable. But cobwebs? Dust? Shredded upholstery? Lamps tipped over and not righted again? Coffee mugs and drinking glasses standing around, the dregs grown over with mold?

"Excuse the way the place looks," Helmers said. He edged between the slumping stacks and sat in the one chair clear for anyone to sit in. "Anybody'd think I was a drunk. I'm not. I'm only drunk on one thing—writing. I get up in the morning, come downstairs and eat some cereal, go to the machine back yonder with a mug of coffee, write, eat supper, watch TV, go to bed, get up in the morning, start the whole routine over again. Hell, sometimes I don't get out of my pajamas from one end of the week to the other. A day off? What's a day off?" He poked around among papers on a table next to the chair, came up with scissors, slit the tape on the carton and pulled open the flaps. "I haven't got time to clean house, and if I had time, my bad back and short wind wouldn't let me." He took out a book with a very shiny jacket, found a pen in the rubble, scrawled on the flyleaf, clapped the cover closed, and handed the book to Dave. "Now you're right up to date," he said.

"I'll read it with pleasure." Dave turned for the door. The place made him so sad he couldn't wait to get away. "And I'll have Kevin Nakamura deliver your car this afternoon." But Helmers had already pushed up out of the chair and was heading at his wounded bear's walk for a back room, struggling to shed his jacket as he went. Through the door he opened, Dave glimpsed paper chaos, overflowing file cabinets, more teetery stacks of books, and the shapes of a computer, a monitor, a printer, all of them dusty and finger-smeared.

"Thanks," Helmers called. "Good seeing you, Dave." And he closed the door behind him.

The little witness had had a bath when Dave got to Madge's big white house on the beach. She'd put him in a paisley pajama top and tied it at the waist with a flower-print scarf. He was pale and runty, with a mop of black hair and wide no-color eyes, and there was an ugly bruise on one cheekbone, but he looked very clean. He stood, sipping berry juice from a small carton, and looking out one of the broad windows of Madge's immense white living room at the beach and the blue, sun-glittering Pacific. Surfers teetered on incoming breakers. Out yonder, sailboats tilted.

Dave said, "Hi. I'm Dave. I've brought you some clothes." He walked to the boy, crouched, opened the sack, drew out a red jogging suit. "This color okay?"

"She threw away my underwear," the boy said.

"Don't worry," Dave said. "Here's new underwear." He tore the plastic wrappers off the packages of shorts and T-shirts. "Go ahead, put them on."

The boy looked past him at tall, gaunt, lantern-jawed Madge standing in the middle of the room watching them. Madge laughed, and went away, saying, "I won't look."

"What's your name?" Dave said.

"Zach." The boy untied the red scarf and wiggled the shirt off his bony shoulders and let it fall to the deep white carpet, and got into the shorts and the T-shirt. "It was Rachel who took me, but she fell asleep and I ran away."

"Took you from where?" Dave used his penknife to cut the price tags off the jogging togs. He laid the tags and strings and plastic stems in a white ashtray on a white table. "From home?"

The boy pulled the small soft trousers on. Watching Dave tie the drawstring for him, he nodded. "Home."

Dave asked, "Where is that?"

"Where I live." Zach said it as if it ought to be obvious. He took the shirt and pulled it on over his head. The outfit was a little too large. Dave was less than expert on children's sizes. So was Helmers. He and Katherine had had a child—but that was long ago. He'd been no help. The boy said, "We went to a motel. She said she had to think." He reached into the bag and drew out white tube socks with red and blue trim. He sat down and pulled these onto his feet. "But she fell asleep."

Dave handed him small red-and-white jogging shoes. "Can you tell me where you live?"

Zach studied the shoes. "She had a gun." He put the shoes on. By blind chance, they seemed to fit.

Dave laced them up and tied them for him. "Rachel, you mean?" He got to his feet, muscles painful, joints stiff.

"I heard a bang, and I ran to see, and this man was laying in the breezeway, and when she saw me she put the gun in her purse and grabbed me and we ran and got in her car. We drove around and around a long time. And then she stopped and put me in the trunk."

Dave put out a hand to touch the bruise and Zach flinched away. Dave said, "Did she do that?"

"No," Zach said. "I fell and hurt myself. Before. I'm always falling and hurting myself." Zach had set the little carton of juice on the windowsill. He got it again and sipped through the straw for a moment. Then he said, "I go around by myself at night." He giggled. "Tessa doesn't know. She says how can I hurt myself asleep in my bed."

"Go around where—the neighborhood?"

Zach shook his head. "The apartments. Outdoors. It's very big. There's good places to hide nobody knows but me."

"Who's Tessa—your mother?"

"Of course." Again, Zach was a little scornful at how ignorant Dave was. "Len's my father. He's a hardhat." Zach patted the top of his head.

"And what's his last name?" Dave said.

Zach sucked at the straw again, but the carton was empty. "Len," he said.

"Do you know your telephone number?"

Zach looked around him. "I go to the Toyland School."

"And where is that?" Dave said.

"Los Angeles, California, U.S.A.," Zach said.

"Tessa and Len must be looking for you," Dave said. "Maybe they called the police. I've got a friend on the—"

"We don't call the police," Zach said.

Madge took Zach by the hand up a white staircase to her studio of long white drafting tables and swirling colors. Madge was as old as Dave, but she'd never given up her pursuit of sex with the ideal girl. None of her sunburned, bouncy assistants lasted long, yet it seemed to Dave she was losing her heart to a new one every time he saw her. Today's was called Lauren, and her surprised and cheery cries of welcome to Zach rang down the stairs. Dave sank into one of the big square white chairs in the living room and rang Lieutenant Jefferson

14

Leppard of LAPD's homicide division in the glass house downtown. He was on uneasy terms with Leppard. He'd outfoxed an officer Leppard had set to protect him on a case where Dave refused to put the man's life at risk. But now that Ken Barker, Dave's friendly enemy in the department for thirty years, had retired, Dave had to make do with Leppard. He liked the black officer, a high-style dresser with a wry sense of humor—and he wished he'd lighten up. Given time, maybe he would. Unless Dave crossed him again.

He sounded sore. "What is it, Brandstetter? I thought you'd retired. I thought I could breathe easy at last."

"Did you have a homicide last night? A shooting?"

"Gang drive-by?" Leppard said. "Three of them."

"Not a gang drive-by. I don't think so. Try a large apartment complex somewhere. Probably not too affluent."

"Cricket Shales," Leppard said. "Ex-pop guitarist, busted eighteen months back for dealing drugs, just out of San Quentin. Shot with a thirty-two, out near Culver City. He had little plastic envelopes of crack in his pockets."

"I have a witness," Dave said. "Only a little kid, but a witness. A friend of mine in Malibu was out walking on the beach at dawn. She's not an exercise fiend, she's a romantic. It's a nice unpeopled time of day, sunrise."

"Perfect for a mugging," Leppard said.

"Not this morning," Dave said. "This morning, here's this grubby little boy."

"Not near Culver City," Leppard said.

"Wait a minute," Dave said. "She asked him where he'd come from, and he said a motel, and pointed at the highway. He'd been kidnapped, but his captor fell asleep, and he got away."

"Active imagination," Leppard said. "Too much TV. Look, we don't need a witness. We know who did it—a young ex-druggie named Rachel Klein. She lives in the apartment complex. Only she's not home this morning, is she? She was Shales's significant other and sparring partner before he went to jail. He probably came back to claim her."

"Rachel—that's what my little witness called her," Dave said. "Rachel. She was bending over the body, holding a gun. She saw him watching her, and grabbed him and took off with him in her car."

"We didn't know that part," Leppard said.

"Who told you the part you do know?"

"Her new boyfriend. A brother by the name of Jordan Vickers—runs a halfway house for junkies, ex-junkies, he likes to hope. She barged in there, woke him up, said she'd stumbled on Cricket shot dead outside her door, and oh, my God, what was she going to do now? He said she ought to have phoned the police right away, but since she hadn't, she should go straight to them now. Offered to take her, go in with her. But she was scared, hysterical. She'd be blamed. Her old connection with Cricket would make her the obvious suspect. No way was she going to the police. She had a gun. He couldn't stop her. She took off, and he phoned us."

"She didn't tell him she had the child with her?"

"He didn't mention it," Leppard said. "He would have. Jordan Vickers is a very righteous dude."

"No missing boy reported from that neighborhood?"

"How old? What's his name?"

"Zach—no last name. I don't know how old. He looks underfed. Spindly little mutt, black shaggy hair, light eyes. Wandering around in the middle of the night all alone in his underwear. Bruise on his cheek. He claims he fell down, but it looks to me like someone hit him. However, maybe that detail wouldn't be in the report. People don't like admitting to the cops they punch out their young."

"Too right," Leppard said grimly. "I'll check with juvenile, but that kind don't always call."

"You sound pretty sure Rachel Klein did the shooting."

"She's been in trouble with the police before—back in her old life with Cricket. Time and again. Possession. Drunk driving. Aiding in the commission of a liquor store holdup. Domestic vi-o-lence."

"Never a dull moment. What about her new life?"

"Vickers claims she's clean, a changed woman. She's been back at her job for over a year, now—office work, some record company. He believes what she told him about finding Cricket there dead. But he doesn't know she held back the truth about snatching your buddy Zach. That's got to look bad, even to him. Especially to him. Like the old Rachel, right? To run and hide—that doesn't make her look guilty enough. No, no—she has to add kidnapping."

"Why self-destruct in a small way?" Dave said.

"Vickers would tell you self-destructive types can be turned around," Leppard said.

"The statistics are against him," Dave said.

"This one is," Leppard said. "Look—you're sure this is a lead? It seems too easy. He really called this woman Rachel, did he?"

"He called her Rachel," Dave said.

"Right. I'm coming down there. Wait for me."

"It will take you at least half an hour," Dave said. "I'll use the time to drive Zach along the coast road. Maybe he'll remember which motel it was."

Madge sat with Zach cuddled against her bony frame in the back of the Jaguar while Dave drove slowly along the shoulder of the coast road. Rocks fallen from the cliff face popped under the tires. Madge kept pointing out the motels to Zach as they hove in view, and in the rearview mirror Dave could see the boy frown, considering them one by one. But each time, he shook his head. It was a good many miles farther on that he said:

"That one. The blue one. With the bird."

The bird was a neon seagull on a tall pole next to the highway. Dave swung the car onto a gravel driveway-parking area. He found a parking slot and switched off the engine. Madge said, marveling, "You walked all the way from here?"

"I ran." Zach nodded. "I didn't want her to catch me again. I didn't want her to put me in the trunk."

Dave opened the car door. "How did you remember the seagull?"

"When she let me out of the trunk, I saw it." He pointed. "There's real ones on the beach."

"I'll be right back." Dave trudged to the glass door pasted over with the logos of credit card companies, and pushed into an office of simulated wood paneling and plastic plants. A pale youngster on crutches smiled at him from behind a counter. His hair was cut spiky. He wore a long T-shirt with a surfer stenciled on it, and flowered shorts that came an inch below the knee. Dave showed him his private investigator's license. "Look at your registrations for last night, please?" The kid blinked, sat down clumsily—one of those new rigs that takes the place of the old plaster cast stiffened his right leg—and tapped buttons on a computer keyboard. A list came up on the monitor, green on black. He tapped another button, a printer ground and keened, the kid ripped off a green-lined sheet and laid it in front of Dave. He dug reading glasses from his jacket pocket and peered at the names. Rachel Klein's was not one of them. But here was an R. Vickers. That would do. He put the reading glasses away and asked the kid, "Were you on duty last night? Three A.M.?"

"I wondered about her," the kid said. "You can usually pick up two, three hours' sleep then, sitting here. Nobody but all-night truckers on the highway, nobody wanting a motel room. And here she came running, knocking at the door. We keep it locked after midnight—want a good look at anybody coming then. Shook up? I thought, "Who you running from, babe?" Good looking, but her hair was all mussed, and her eyes were every place, and she couldn't catch her breath. If she'd offered a check or a credit card, I'd have told her we were full up, sorry. But she had cash, and the VACANCY sign was on outside, and I really couldn't think of an excuse."

"And she was pretty," Dave said.

"Yeah, really." The kid grinned with glorious teeth. "In a bikini, you'd keel over dead. Sheeh!"

Dave turned for the door. "Room one-eighty?"

"She's gone. I don't know when. Before the maids got there. What do you want her for?"

"Kidnapping," Dave said. "And possibly murder."

The kid went pale under his sunburn. "Jesus."

"The little boy got away, and he's okay," Dave said. "But the man is definitely dead."

"Did she have a gun with her?" the kid asked faintly.

"So the little boy says." Dave smiled. "Maybe the reason you didn't see it is that she had cash, right?"

3

THE APARTMENT COMPLEX had seen better days. It took up half a block on a side street between Washington and Jefferson. Cinnamon-brown stucco with black trim, two stories, parking space underneath, gated by heavy steel mesh. The landscaping had grown tall and brushy. The balconies were cluttered with forgotten barbecues, bicycles, bulging plastic sacks. On several, clothes hung over the straight steel railings. Holding Zach's hands, Dave and Leppard walked into a square patio. The first block of apartments opened off this, ground-floor doors you could walk right up to, second-floor doors you climbed outside stairways and walked to along galleries.

"This where you live?" Leppard asked. The boy shook his head.

Leppard raised his eyebrows at Dave. "This is where the shooting happened."

"Here?" Dave looked around for marks on the cement.

"Back there." Leppard led Dave and the boy across the patio and into a second one. There was a third one to the side through a breezeway. That one had a swimming pool, empty except for needles from a Japanese pine that bent over it. Leppard moved toward the breezeway. "Here," he said. Chalk outlined the shape of a human form on the paving. The paving needed sweeping and washing down, and there seemed to be a bloodstain. "Where were you?" Leppard asked Zach.

"There." Zach pointed a stubby finger upwards. To a gallery with apartment doors and windows along it.

"You live up there?" Dave said.

Again Zach shook his head. "I go around at night." He waved both arms. "Everywhere. There used to be more lights, but now it's mostly dark. Nobody can see me. I can hide. There's lots of good places."

"Why do you want to hide?" Leppard said. Zach just stared at him.

"Is there somebody you're afraid of?" Dave said. "The one who hit you and gave you that bruise on your face?"

Zach shook his head. "I fell down. I fall down and hurt myself sometimes."

"That's what you get for going around in the dark," Leppard said. "What were you doing up on that gallery?"

"Going someplace," Zach said.

"To your apartment?" Dave said. "Is it one of those?"

Zach said, "And then I heard the bangs. Bang, bang, bang. And I came down to see."

"And Rachel saw you and took you with her in her car."

Zach nodded. "She brought me a chili dog in the car." He strayed off to play with a padlock on a lean-to Dave figured probably held gardening tools. "And orange soda."

"In the trunk?" Leppard said.

"No. Afterward was when she put me in the trunk." The hasp that held the padlock came loose with a rattle. "She had to talk to somebody." He swung open the doors of the lean-to and peered inside. "She showed me the gun, and said if I made any noise, she'd come shoot me."

Leppard said to Dave, "Wouldn't Vickers love that?"

"So you didn't make any noise?" Dave called.

Zach looked at him again as if he was a fool.

A sharp voice echoed off the walls and galleries. "Zach. Zach Gruber? Is that you? Where the hell have you been?

Len will beat the shit out of you—" A young woman came at a run—brassy dyed hair, too much makeup, too-tight slacks, fake-fur jacket over bulging breasts, bare feet in spike-heeled sandals, toenails brightly painted. Zach had hopped into the lean-to and was pulling the doors shut. She snatched them open, grabbed him, yanked him out. "I been looking all over for you. I was half crazy." She had him by the arm and was propelling him away, his feet in the new jogging shoes barely touching down, when Leppard called:

"Hold it, please, lady. Police officers."

She threw them a look as scared as Zach's had been when he saw her. For a minute, Dave thought she was going to pick Zach up and make a run for it, but she changed her mind. "What for? You brought him home, did you? Where'd you find him? Where'd he get to this time?"

Leppard went to her. "Run away a lot, does he?"

"He—he—" She broke that off, took a breath, worked up a smile. "No, not really. He's a pretty good kid." She gave him a hug. He was like a rag doll, letting her hug him if that was what she wanted. He looked away at nothing. "I've been frantic, is all. You can understand that, can't you?" She searched their faces. Dave twitched her a smile.

"It wasn't his fault this time," he said.

"You ought to teach him his address and telephone number," Leppard said. "And his last name. Gruber?" He looked at Zach. "Your father's last name is Gruber. His full name is Len Gruber. That means your name is Zach Gruber. Now, you're a big enough boy to remember that, aren't you?"

Zach pushed at a crushed cigarette pack with his foot.

Tessa Gruber frowned at Dave. "What do you mean, it wasn't his fault?"

"He didn't go on his own," Dave said. "Someone took him."

Leppard said, "There was a shooting here last night." He pointed with a thumb toward the breezeway. "There."

She looked and saw the chalk marks on the ground and winced. "I didn't know. I work nights." She looked anxiously at her watch. "And I'm going to be late if I don't get moving. Listen, thanks for finding him." She grabbed Zach's arm roughly and started off with him. "I've been out looking for you since breakfast."

Leppard walked after her. "We found him at the beach. Malibu." That stopped Tessa. She turned back, surprised. Zach skipped off out of sight. Leppard went on, "A young woman neighbor of yours took Zach down there. After the shooting. He came running here when he heard the shots and he saw her. Her name is Rachel Klein. Zach seems to know her. What about you? Apartment one-oh-seven-two."

She shook her head. Quickly. Maybe too quickly. "Never heard of her. There's a lot of apartments in this place, lot of people. Most of them I've never even seen."

"You don't seem very curious," Dave said.

"About what?" she said. "If I don't get to Shadows by four, Mr. Zinneman could fire me. Then there'll be two of us out of work. What will we eat on? How'll we pay the God damn fantasyland rent here? Zach, where are you? I haven't got time to be curious. What am I supposed to be curious about?"

"About who was shot," Dave said.

She snorted. "People get shot in this neighborhood all the time. It was bound to happen inside here sooner or later. Management won't fix the outdoor lighting. It's drugs, isn't it? He was a crack dealer, right?"

"Right," Leppard said. "Name of Cricket Shales."

Dave thought he saw fright in her eyes, but her face was blank, and she said in the steadiest of voices, "Never heard of him. Weird name. Look, I really gotta go now. Zach, you come here, right now." Zach came, dragging his feet.

"We'll trail along," Leppard said. "Your husband home?"

She glanced wryly over her shoulder as she prodded Zach ahead of her. "You think he'd help me look for the kid? He's got television to watch. He didn't watch television"—she climbed stairs—"it would go out of business, wouldn't it?" She zigzagged past beach balls and spider bikes and skateboards along a balcony to a door she flung open. She pushed Zach inside. "You know where he was? At the fucking beach. Cops brought him home."

Dave and Leppard went along the gallery after her. They heard her say, "No, Len, not now. They're right behind me. They want to talk to you. I gotta get ready for work." An inner door banged. Leppard and Dave stepped into a blank-walled room of meaningless furniture and lamps where a muscular, unshaven young man in ragged jeans sat in an easy chair with a beer can and a bag of potato chips, and stared at a noisy television set. The images were of men shooting at each other in a warehouse.

Leppard picked up the remote control from the chair arm and switched off the set. "Your son was kidnapped, Mr. Gruber. By a young woman who lives in these buildings. Her name is Rachel Klein. Do you know her?"

Gruber reached for the remote in Leppard's hand. "Give me that. You got no right—" Leppard dropped the remote into his jacket pocket. It was a stunning jacket. The tweed was woven in some tumbledown cottage in the Scots highlands, seeds and grasses still caught in the wool.

"I'd like to hear your answers."

"Hell, I didn't do nothin'. Ask this Ruby Shine."

"Rachel Klein. We can't find her. Where is she?"

"How the hell would I know? I never heard of her."

"Zach knows her. Young, attractive? A neighbor?"

"Look—I don't chase women, okay? I got a wife other men would kill themselves to get. And I'd kill them if they tried. I don't chase women." He squinted at Leppard. "What did she kidnap Zach for? Shit, we haven't got any money."

"He was a witness," Leppard said. "Your wife was at work. Where were you last night?"

Gruber straightened up in the chair. His feet, bare, the soles dirty, had been up on an ottoman. He put them on the floor. "What the hell does that mean?"

"Only that there was a shooting out there." Leppard jerked his head. "That's what Zach was a witness to. I wondered if you heard the shots."

"I didn't hear nothin'. What time?"

"Preliminary medical report puts it at midnight."

"Midnight?" Gruber laughed. "I was in bed asleep. All right, passed out. Three six-packs. Tessa says I'm turning into a pig. Sweet talk, right? Hell, you try being without a job for five months. A man loses his self-respect. I drink too much. That's my problem." He put the fascinating subject of himself aside and woke up to what Leppard had said. "Preliminary medical? That don't mean a shooting. That means the guy was killed, don't it?"

"Who said it was a guy?" Leppard asked.

"Oh, Christ." Gruber made a face. "All right. The woman, then. Whoever it is, they're dead, right?"

Leppard nodded. "Cricket Shales. You know him?"

Gruber slumped quickly back in the chair again. "No." Without looking at Leppard, he stretched out a hand to him. "Now, can I have my remote back, officer, please, sir?"

"What's wrong with you, Gruber? Your son was kidnapped. Where's your humanity? You didn't even report him missing."

Gruber blinked at him. "He's back. He's okay. What do you want from me?"

Dave said, "That bruise on his face doesn't worry you?"

Gruber shrugged. "Dame probably hit him. He can get on your nerves."

"Hit him yourself, sometimes, do you?" Dave said.

Gruber glanced at him. "You got any kids?"

"No," Dave said.

"I didn't think so," Gruber said, "or you wouldn't ask."

Leppard said, "Where'd he go now?" and left the room.

"How the hell do I know?" Gruber got up, stepped to the television set, and switched it on. On the tube, a dog in the back of a parked pickup truck was looking longingly into the bed of the red pickup truck parked next to it. At last, the dog hopped from his truck into the new one. Of a different brand, of course. Dave wondered if the message was "Let your dog choose your next truck." Voices reached him.

Tessa Gruber yelped, "Where are you taking him?"

"Downtown," Leppard answered, "to police headquarters."

"You can't," she said. "Zach, come here."

Zach didn't do that. He came into the living room, hanging onto Leppard's hand. She came after them. She'd put on a black cocktail waitress's outfit, very short skirt, net stockings. She had good legs. She shrilled at Gruber, "You going to let them do this?"

"I guess they want a medic to check him out." Gruber stared at the television set. "See if he's okay. They do that after kidnappings." He took up his beer can and gulped from it. "It's routine, Tessa. You'd know stuff like that if you ever watched the news."

"Well, you go with them," she said.

"Come on," he protested. "What for?"

"Because I can't go, stupid. I gotta get to work."

Leppard passed the remote back to Gruber and went with Zach by the hand to the front door. "He'll be all right." Dave opened the door and stepped onto the gallery. Leppard did this, too, then turned back to say, "But don't take any trips, Mr. Gruber, please. We may want to talk to you later." He started off along the gallery.

"Get off my case," Gruber said. "I got enough trouble."

"Wait." Tessa trotted after them. "How long you going to keep him? When'll you bring him back?"

"Do you really give a damn?" Leppard said.

"What? I looked for him all day. I told you."

"Maybe, but you didn't report him missing," Leppard said. "The juvenile authorities are going to hold that against you." He sighed regretfully and, wagging his round, sleek head, he started off again, making for the stairs. "They may not ever let me bring him back."

She didn't grab for Zach, go for Leppard with her nails, or wail, or curse. She just stood and watched them go. When Dave halted on the far side of the patio below, and looked back, she was still up there in her sleazy, sexy costume, gazing at them mutely and without expression.

He said to Leppard, "Bible student, are you?"

Leppard chuckled and led Zach toward the street. "You talking about King Solomon?"

"He somehow leaps to mind," Dave said.

4

THE TOYLAND SCHOOL was on Venice near La Cienega—flat-roofed, pale green stucco buildings, construction-paper daffodils Cellotaped inside the windows. Outside in a gravel play yard stood a short chute, swings, a jungle gym to climb on, a steel barrel to crawl through, a little train with two cars behind it on a circle of track, all these things painted bright red, blue, yellow, green. A high chain-link fence enclosed the yard. The latch on the gate was up out of the reach of small fry. And when Dave walked up to it, a young Asian woman in jeans, a blouse, a cardigan, was standing on tiptoe, stretching her arms to put a padlock in the latch.

He asked, "May I help?"

She was startled for a second. It wasn't a spot where you'd expect passers-by on foot. The sidewalk never got used. Here in front of the school it was swept—but along Venice in both directions nobody had paid any attention to it for some time. Warehouses, an auto repair shop, a screen-door maker, a sign painter—clean sidewalks didn't affect their profits. She blinked up at him through blue-rimmed glasses, studying him, her head tilted. It appeared he passed muster. She smiled and put the lock into his hand. "Please. I'd be grateful." She stepped aside. "It's a nuisance to be so short. If I'd been born here, it would be different. Now, in Japan the children are growing up on hamburgers and pizzas, and they'll all be tall as Americans."

Fastening the padlock, Dave started to cite the caterpillar in *Alice's Adventures in Wonderland* who indignantly claimed that two inches was quite a good height, indeed, then thought better of it. "My name is Brandstetter." He took from his inside jacket pocket the ostrich-hide folder that held his private investigator's license, and showed it to her. "I'm working with the police. The case involves a child who comes here. Zach Gruber."

"Oh, dear." She peered up at him, eyes anxious. "Has anything happened to him? Is he all right?"

"A lot has happened to him." Dave put the folder away. "But aside from a bruise on his face, I don't think he's hurt." He glanced at the buildings. "You're—?"

"Celia Yamashita," she said. "It's my school."

Dave said, "A shooting took place at Zach's apartment complex last night, he saw someone standing over the victim, and that someone saw him and kidnapped him." The schoolmistress put a hand to her forehead. He said, "Don't be upset. He got away, a friend of mine scooped him up off the beach and called the police, and he's safe now—"

"But doesn't that explain the bruise?" she said.

"He claims not, says he fell down earlier, and banged his face. He's accident-prone. It happens all the time."

"'This is a recorded message,'" she said grimly.

"He's come to school battered, has he?"

"The first time, he claimed he'd fallen down stairs. I phoned his home, couldn't reach anyone, so I took him to my doctor. He didn't think it was a fall, but he couldn't be sure what had happened."

"And the second time?" Dave said.

"He was a sight. He said his mother stopped the car suddenly to avoid a collision, and he banged his face on the glove compartment." Celia Yamashita glanced at her watch, picked up a shoulder bag from the sidewalk, started away. Dave strolled along beside her. She went on, "This time I thought Child Welfare better know about it. They interviewed Zach and then they talked to the parents. Nothing. The neighbors couldn't contribute anything. That Mr. Gruber drinks and gets loud and verbally abusive sometimes and she screams at him—nothing about child abuse."

"But you're not convinced?" Dave said.

She threw him a glum smile. "I'm not convinced. And neither are you, Mr. Brandstetter, or you wouldn't be here."

"Does he fall asleep a lot during the days?"

She cocked her head. "How did you know?"

"He seems to spend his nights wandering around the apartment complex, and he keeps saying there are good hiding places there. But he won't say why that's important to him—who it is he wants to hide from."

"He keeps things to himself."

"Frightened into silence?"

"I wouldn't be surprised." They'd gone down a gritty alley of abandoned auto carcasses. Behind the school, she unlocked a Japanese economy car. "And something else. He never cries. All the children have little mishaps. If he hurts himself, or someone hurts him—not a sound, not a tear. So, whatever the neighbors say, I think his father abuses him and threatens him with worse if he cries, so of course, no one hears." Celia Yamashita tossed her bag into the car. "As for his mother—well, what can you say? She's a waitress at a cocktail bar. They're"—she blinked into the westering sunlight while she groped for words— "not exactly parenting material, are they?" She got into the little car, slammed the door, peered out at him, worrying the subject some more. "I mean, one day—not long after she first brought Zach here—she sent a man from the bar to pick him up after school. A musician in torn jeans and long hair. Not a responsible-looking person. Very strange eyes. I hated letting him take Zach, really, but she'd phoned ahead. It was an emergency. And Zach seemed to know him and trust him."

"A guitarist?" Dave said. "Name of Cricket?"

She started the car. "That's the one. Cricket."

He reached the canyon house at sunset, dog-tired. This happened to him nowadays. He wasn't sure why. He was sure he didn't want to know why. Scarcely noticing the red roadster parked beside him, he climbed out of the Jaguar, locked it, went around the front building into the courtyard sheltered by the old oak—and stopped. The cookshack windows glowed with light. He pulled the screen door, pushed the wooden door, and Amanda smiled at him from the massive old farmhouse stove where she was cooking, wrapped in a yellow apron.

Neatly made, not yet forty, pretty and bright and tiny, she was of all unlikely things Dave's stepmother, Carl Brandstetter's widow, widow number nine.

The first, Dave's mother, was long dead. Dave didn't remember her. Of the others he'd seen little once Carl had shed them, trailing jewelry, Paris gowns, and money. Most had shown up for the great man's funeral, a few years back. It had been quite a crowd. How different they'd been from each other. No one could accuse Carl Brandstetter of marrying the same woman over and over again. Quite the reverse. Dave remembered some of them kindly. To most of them, even when he was small and lived at home, he'd been as dim a presence as they'd been to him.

Young and lovely as she was, and deeply in love with Carl, Amanda might not have lasted, either. In more than seventy years of living, Carl had never got the hang of constancy. But he hadn't been given time to tire of Amanda. Late one night, only a few short years into their marriage, while driving ninety miles an hour on a freeway, he'd had a heart attack, and totaled his Bentley and himself—and so Amanda became widow of record.

Lost and forlorn, wandering aimless through the handsome, heartlessly empty rooms of a sprawling Beverly Hills mansion, Amanda had needed something to do with her time, and Dave had asked her to revamp these shacky stable buildings into livable quarters. She'd done a smart job, and with Madge Dunstan's seconding, he'd got her to set up in business on Rodeo Drive, where she'd prospered and made a name for herself. Picture spreads of her work had been in all the glossy shelter magazines. More importantly, she'd become Dave's friend.

"Dave, I'm so glad." She opened a massive old oak icebox in which she'd concealed the works of a state-of-the-art refrigerator, and lifted out of it a misty pitcher and a frosty glass. While she poured a martini for him, she said, "Dave Brandstetter, Cliff Callahan." She meant a giant of a boy who sat on a chair at the big scrubbed deal table in the middle of the room. He rose and held out a huge, very clean hand. His blue eyes twinkled. His voice rumbled from a chest that stretched hell out of the cloth on what ought to have been a roomy shirt.

"How are you, Mr. Brandstetter? Good to know you." He crushed Dave's hand when he shook it. "Amanda thinks the world of you. She talks about you all the time. We're going to get married."

"This is a surprise," Dave said to Amanda.

She stood on tiptoe and kissed his cheek. "I wanted you to be the first to know, and I didn't want it to be on the phone. Anyway, your phone is always unplugged. So I took a chance on your being home tonight." She put the icy glass in his hand. "I was counting on your promise not to sneak out of retirement again." Her look was suspicious. "You haven't, have you?"

Dave sat at the table. "It's touch and go. I promised Cecil I wouldn't. I'd like to keep that promise, but—" He shrugged, and sipped the martini. It would probably knock him out. That's what martinis were doing to him lately. But he wasn't going to admit this now. Besides, it tasted good. "This is glorious," he told her. "Thank you." Very casually, he got up, went to a drawer, took out a pack of Marlboros. Amanda was busy making salad dressing and didn't notice. He sat down again, quickly opened the pack, lit a cigarette, and was so relieved to have smoke in his lungs once more he almost wept. He sipped the martini and said, "You like children, Mr. Callahan?"

Callahan was blond, with skin like a girl's. He blushed and gave Amanda a sheepish glance. "We haven't talked about it yet."

"Dave," Amanda said, "what a question."

"Madge found a small runaway boy called Zach Gruber on her stretch of beach this morning. It looks as if his father beats him. I think so, the woman who runs his preschool thinks so. And so does Jeff Leppard, which means little Zach is very likely going to end up in a foster home. And that means a succession of foster homes for years and years. Sometimes that works out. But not often. Today's world is hard enough to survive in even for kids with parents who stick around and treat them kindly."

Amanda was back at the stove. Whatever she'd concocted there filled the air with tantalizing smells. "No—we're not candidates for adoption. Not yet."

Now Dave remembered where he'd glimpsed Callahan. On television. In a series about a daredevil young electronics whiz with an advanced-state helicopter called Icarus that he kept hidden in improbable quarters, slumland warehouse on the outside, magical palace full of winking, beeping electronics on the inside, and which helped him solve crimes, destroy evildoers, and rescue maidens in distress. He said to Callahan, "I expect Zach is a fan of yours."

"He'd be disappointed," Callahan said, "when he looked around my digs and couldn't find Icarus." He laughed. "Or even one computer. Hell, I can't figure out how to hitch up my VCR. Don't tell anybody, but I can't even drive a car."

Dave laughed. "I didn't know they hired actors like that. Not anymore. What happened to "Cut to the chase"?"

"I'm no actor," Callahan said. "I'm somebody big and good-looking that moves when the director says move, and speaks when the writer gives me words, while people who know what they're doing take my picture and record my voice."

Dave liked Callahan. "Don't let it bother you. An interviewer asked good old Kate Hepburn the other day to explain her success. "Cheekbones," she said.

Callahan laughed. And Cecil came in. His face lit up. "Ah, you're not out chasing kidnappers." Then he frowned. "You're smoking."

"Not my fault," Dave said. "Amanda made martinis. No way can I drink a martini without a cigarette. Cecil Harris, this is Cliff Callahan. I expect it's only brag, but he claims he's going to marry our Amanda."

"Whoa," Cecil said with a grin, holding out his hand. "Without my permission? I am her father, you know."

Callahan said, "That explains why she's so tall."

"I'm crouching so as not to embarrass you," she said.

"I think I'm going to like being part of this family," Callahan said.

"Have to be at the studio at six." Callahan yawned, stretched, got up from the hearth where he'd been sitting. A Scrabble board was on the hearth. The four of them had surrounded it, two in wing chairs, two seated on the bricks, laughing, squabbling, jumping up to check each others' doubtful spellings in three massive dictionaries that lay open on the long corduroy couch. Callahan found his jacket on the hat tree beside the bar at the shadowy far end of the room. "Sorry to tear you away so early, sweetheart, but that's the actor's life."

Dave touched Amanda before she could get up, and told Callahan, "I'll be your chauffeur." He got to his feet. "It's a condo at the marina, is it?"

Callahan came back into the lamplight. "The housebreaker's garden of earthly delights," he said.

35

"Aren't you tired?" Cecil looked up at Dave doubtfully. "Don't you want me to do it?"

"You stay and outpoint Amanda." Dave's jacket lay over an arm of the couch. He picked it up. "You're the literary gent around here."

Cecil scoffed. "I write news copy for TV, and that makes me the literary gent?"

"The nearest thing our team has got." Dave felt in his pocket for keys and cigarettes, and headed for the door. "I'll be back."

"I don't trust you," Cecil said. "You're going snooping about that little kid."

"Absolutely not." He was going snooping about the little kid's parents. He opened the door, stepped out, Callahan after him, and called back, "Scout's honor."

"All you've got is an hour," Cecil shouted. "Then I'll call the LAPD to start looking for you."

Dave took long strides across the uneven bricks of the courtyard, pretending he hadn't heard.

Shadows was on Venice in Mar Vista, on the ground floor of a two-story stucco business building freshly painted white. He'd expected something shabby. Shadows wasn't smart, but its sign had all its letters. The banner that read Steaks Lobster Entertainment was clean and new. The little arched dark-green-and-white canvas marquee over the sidewalk wasn't ragged or faded. The parking lot next to the place was mostly empty. The few cars must belong to dawdling diners. The drinkers wouldn't put in an appearance until later. It was early, nine-thirty. It had to be early.

Just after dinner, while Cecil, Amanda, and Callahan were washing up the dishes, laughing, singing snatches of songs Dave didn't know, he had slipped unnoticed over to the rear building to sit at his desk, and telephone the LAPD. Jeff Leppard had left, but Dave arranged with Joey Samuels to haul Tessa and Len Gruber downtown for a talk about Zach. Samuels had agreed, but he couldn't keep them forever. Tessa worried about losing her job. She'd be back at Shadows, wouldn't she, as soon as she could break away? And Dave mustn't be there when she arrived.

The door was carved, painted forest green, and had a big, bronze handle. He pushed it and went inside. Shadows was the right name. The place specialized in those. There were the expected tables, the expected bar—long enough and equipped with enough bottles to show that booze was the essential business of the place, not food. Diners sat at some far tables, men in dark suits, women in freshly set hair and twinkly necklaces—people who worked nine-to-five jobs, treating themselves to a rare night out—dallying with coffee and liqueurs among crumpled napkins. They seemed happy, a little drunk, and sleepy. They'd be leaving soon, before the music started. That would draw a younger crowd. A baby grand piano, chairs, loudspeakers stood on a little stage draped in dark green velveteen, waiting for the band.

Dave sat at the bar on a stool deeply cushioned in dark green simulated leather. Leather padding for elbows edged the bar. The bartender was a middle-aged Hispanic of comfortable girth, brisk if easy motions, a ruffled shirt front, green leather vest. Dave ordered Glenlivet and looked around. There seemed no side exit to the parking lot. A distant, dimly lit hallway showed him pay telephones and a discreet sign: RESTROOMS. There'd be no door to the outside there. He turned his head. Over at the other end of the room glinted the kitchen swinging door. If Tessa arrived before he'd finished here, he'd leave through the kitchen and out the back way. He tilted his head to the bartender, and moved to the other end of the bar. The man brought him his drink, and Dave asked him:

"Mr. Zinneman in tonight?"

The bartender studied him. "Something wrong, sir?"

"I don't think so." Dave showed him his license. The bartender took it doubtfully, held it where the tiny lights that sparkled on the back bar bottles lit it up enough for him to read it. He raised his eyebrows, blinked, handed the folder back to Dave. Dave put it away.

The bartender said, "You sure as hell don't dress like any private nose I ever saw. That suit's handmade."

"I nose for insurance companies," Dave said. "Insurance companies are very rich."

"What do you do—take a percentage?"

"Like a jockey," Dave said. "I just need to ask Mr. Zinneman a few routine questions about Cricket Shales. He used to work here. A musician."

The bartender scoffed, "Don't tell me he had insurance. Who the hell sold it to him? Idiots of Omaha? He's in trouble again, right?"

"The worst possible kind." Dave tried the whiskey. It was not Glenlivet, but he doubted it would help to say so. He supposed he was lucky Shadows stocked malt whiskey at all. This was a Jim Beam shop. He said, "He's dead."

"Dead? He was a young guy. What's he dead from?"

"Bullets. Does that surprise you?"

"Excuse me." The bartender moved off to talk to a small shrunken man whose hatchet nose, thrusting cheekbones, sunken eyes gave him the look of an Egyptian mummy. He had arrived behind the bar from nowhere. Outfitted in a stiff, ill-fitting black suit that could have costumed a small-town deacon in a 1935 movie, he came and shook Dave's hand and said that he was Zinneman, the owner of this unchurchly place. "I understand Cricket Shales has been murdered. That's too bad. He was a talented boy."

"He had a talent for trouble," Dave said. "Can I buy you a drink, Mr. Zinneman?"

Zinneman smiled sadly. "Thank you. I have never been a drinker." He came around and climbed up on the stool next to Dave. "I tried champagne once, at my sister's wedding, when I was sixteen." He straightened the creases in his trousers. "It made me dizzy and sick to my stomach." He brushed imaginary lint off a jacket sleeve. "I decided alcohol was not for me."

"That's an odd confession for a bar owner," Dave said. "Or perhaps it's the restaurant side of the business that attracts you?" The man weighed less than a hundred pounds. Dave gave him a little smile. "Love good food, do you?"

Zinneman laughed. "Borscht and black bread. No, Mr. Bankov, I bought Shadows when I bought the building. I buy and sell buildings. Ordinarily, they are vacant, the businesses that owned them have failed. With Shadows it was different. Shadows had been here a long time. It was prospering. It seemed a shame to close it down. So I became a restaurant owner. I'm not sorry. It has kept me young."

Dave looked at his watch. "You know Shales had been in prison? For drug dealing?"

Zinneman shook his head glumly. "The drug dealing was why I had to fire him. He was selling cocaine, here, in the restaurant. He was a first-rate guitarist, a nice singer. People liked him. He was wonderful for business, but"—he lifted and let fall brown parchment hands—"I could not have law-breaking. I might have lost my liquor license."

"You did the right thing," Dave said. "The law caught up to him. He did eighteen months in San Quentin. When he came out, he headed straight for Rachel Klein's apartment."

"Ah, Rachel." The old man shook his head. "A tragedy. Such a wonderful voice, you know, beautiful. It was here she met Cricket. It was love at first sight. Everyone saw. And soon he was asking her up on the stage to sing. It thrilled her. A lovely girl, too, such nice manners. But"—he sighed—"in only a few months she was drinking heavily, using drugs, neglecting her looks, her clothes. She grew loud and obscene and abusive. People began leaving when they saw her come in. I had to tell Cricket to keep her away."

"They lived together," Dave said.

"I suppose so," Zinneman said. "Young people today—"

"I'm told he was the one who got her onto drugs."

Zinneman said bleakly, "Was that how it was?"

"It appears he came back to start over with her last night," Dave said, "and she shot him." Zinneman was horrified.

"Rachel? I can't believe it."

"She had a new boyfriend, a new life," Dave said. "Cricket must have represented a past she didn't want to be dragged back to. That's how it looks."

"They have her in custody, the police?"

"They can't find her. Where would she go to hide? Can you remember any friends she used to come here with?"

Zinneman frowned to himself. "There was one young woman. Karen? It seems to me they worked together. I believe for some record company." He nodded. "That was it. 'Say What?' That was the name. 'Say What?'"

Dave read his watch again. "It's not proven that she shot Shales, but she did kidnap Zach Gruber."

Zinneman looked at him, startled. "Little Zach? Why?"

Dave told him why. "Later he got away. He's safe now."

"How strange Tessa told me nothing of this."

"What excuse did she give for taking time off tonight?"

Zinneman laughed dryly and waved a hand. "Who listens? Such stories are never the truth. Where is she?"

"Down at police headquarters," Dave said, "settling things about Zach. The police suspect his father of abusing him, beating him. You ever hear anything like that?"

"No, but I am not surprised. I know Len Gruber, and he is a violent man. One night he nearly killed Cricket Shales in here. With his bare hands."

"Is that so? What was his reason?"

"He thought Cricket was having an affair with Tessa." Zinneman shook his head. "It wasn't true, of course. I have observed Tessa for years. This was before Rachel, and perhaps Cricket did want Tessa—most men do. But she scarcely notices. She is in love with only one man—her husband. But he is a stupid boy, fiercely jealous, with a temper like a wild animal. I can't see Rachel killing Cricket. She had loved him too much. But Len Gruber? If he thought Cricket had come back last night for Tessa, he would have killed him in a minute."

5

CECIL SAID, "YOU were staggering when you got here."

"I only had one drink," Dave said.

"I didn't say drunk. Exhausted. Dave—you didn't know where you were." He set a Mexican tin tray on the bedside table. On the tray coffee steamed in big brown pottery mugs. Glasses of orange juice stood beside these. In a basket, a yellow napkin covered what Dave's nose told him were cornmeal muffins. "You didn't know who I was. Or Amanda, either."

"Kept going too long yesterday." Dave sat up groggily in the broad bed on the sleeping loft. The leaf-strewn skylight was open. The sky beyond it was blue. Warm air came in. He stretched cautiously, feeling reminders in his muscles of old injuries that would never quite heal. He squinted at the red LED numerals of the clock. "Jesus—noon already? How come you're not at work?"

"I'll hang around here today." Cecil said this too casually. In stone-washed blue jeans with many pockets, and a fragment of a white tank top, cut off just at the sternum line, he wandered around to the far side of the bed, and switched on the stereo. Horowitz played Scriabin etudes. Horowitz had died the other day, and for now radio was forgetting that there had ever been another pianist. "Nothing pressing at Channel Three. Keep an eye on you."

"Good Lord." Dave swung his feet to the floor. "I'm all right." He pushed to his feet, flapped into his blue corduroy robe. "I don't need around-the-clock nursing." He started down the stairs. But he felt feeble, and held onto the raw pine two-by-four that was the banister. "Not yet. I'm old, but not that old."

"Just take it easy today," Cecil called after him. "That's all I ask. Tomorrow, we'll see how you feel."

Dave grunted, went into the bathroom, shut the door.

When he came out, Cecil was sitting in one of the wing chairs, a long lean leg hooked over the arm, reading the morning *LA Times*. He had brought the tray to the coffee table between the couch and the fireplace. Dave sat on the couch, swallowed the orange juice, tried the coffee. "Can I ask you to get my cigarettes?"

"I'm not helping you kill yourself," Cecil said.

"Climbing the stairs could kill me quicker," Dave said.

Cecil threw down the paper and climbed the stairs and brought back cigarettes and Dave's slim steel lighter. He laid them down with great carefulness to show that he was keeping his temper. He picked up the paper, sat down, and said, "You better see a doctor."

"I promise to obey you. Today, anyway." Dave gave him a smile through blue smoke. "But no doctor, okay?"

"Your father died of a heart attack," Cecil said. "It runs in families. You getting tired this way—it doesn't sound good, it's ominous, all right? There are procedures they can use now on hearts that try shutting down."

"Balloons belong in the hands of children at circuses," Dave said, "not shoved up old men's arteries."

Cecil opened his mouth, closed it again firmly, looked away. He laid the paper on the hearth, picked up his coffee mug and drank from it. He leaned forward in the chair. "Dave—I'm sorry Max died. And all the others in your life that aren't here anymore. But, damn it, grieving won't bring them back. And I'm here, Dave. And I love you. Doesn't that matter?" Tears brightened his eyes. "You can't die on me. What kind of life would I have then?"

"A heart attack can be neat," Dave said. "I'd hate wasting away, being bedridden, a wheelchair case. I can tell you for sure that looking after a foul-tempered old man being eaten up by cancer is not the kind of life I want for you."

"Jesus, what a morning." Cecil jumped up and went to one of the windows box-framed by the bookshelves. It stood open. A branch from one of the untrimmed shrubs outside reached in. He snatched a handful of leaves. "If you can feel better and live a normal life by going to a doctor and getting your heart patched up, why, why, why do you act this way? Hate me. That's all I can see in it."

"It doesn't have to be a bad morning," Dave said. "We can change the subject. I don't know that there's anything wrong with my heart to be fixed. That's your idea."

"You didn't see yourself last night."

Dave took a warm, buttery cornmeal muffin from the basket and held it out. "Come eat this. Comfort food. Isn't that why you made it?"

Cecil dropped the leaves out the window, came back, took the muffin, studied it. "I made it because I have figured out something science doesn't yet know." He sat down, bit into the muffin, hummed happily, licked his fingers, drank some coffee. "That corn doesn't damage the heart the way wheat does. North Americans eat wheat flour. Aztecs ate cornmeal, *masa.* You ever see those pyramids they built in the jungles down there? A hundred feet high? Steps all the way to the top? No bad hearts among those people."

"Brilliant." Dave ate a muffin himself. Drinking coffee, smoking, he said, "Did the phone ring earlier?"

Cecil was working on another muffin. He nodded. When he'd got the muffin down, he said, "Joey Samuels. He said the police released Zach to his loving parents last night. Juvenile thinks he got bruised during the kidnapping."

"*Zach* doesn't think so," Dave said.

"Aren't experts wonderful?" Cecil said.

"I'll let you know when I meet one," Dave said.

He toiled back up to the loft and slept again. At three thirty he awoke. The afternoon was warm. Dim sounds of music reached him. Mostly thudding bass. From the front building. Cecil and Dave agreed on Bach and Bartok, Mahler and Mozart, Bellini and Berg. And on jazz—they both liked it suave, Bix Beiderbecke, Johnny Hodges, Lionel Hampton. But on rock they did not see eye to eye. Cecil bought armfuls of CDs by groups with outlandish names, clothes, haircuts, and listened to them by himself, driving to and from work in his van. He went to monstrous concerts in vast arenas with friends his own age from Channel Three—Jesus Salcido, Curly Ravitch, Billy Choy. At home, he rarely played rock unless Dave was away. Today, Dave might as well be away—and, time on his hands, that appeared to be what he was doing. Probably dancing. All by himself in that big empty building. Picturing it made Dave sad. But he hadn't the energy to go to him and be company for him. Certainly not to dance. Wanly, he reached for the telephone on the bedside table and rang Jeff Leppard to report what he'd learned at Shadows.

"What are you trying to say?" Leppard asked.

"That Len Gruber is a liar. He did know Cricket. Maybe instead of passing out that night, he looked into Zach's room, saw he was gone, went hunting for him, caught Cricket prowling around, thought he'd come for Tessa, and shot him."

"Where did he get the gun?" Leppard said. "We know Cricket owned a gun, a thirty-two, it was registered, but—"

"Why hadn't he left it behind at Rachel's? It was her place they shared while they lived together. He'd have a key. She wasn't there, maybe he went in and got it and when Gruber surprised him, he pulled it out to protect himself."

"And Gruber took it away from him," Leppard asked, "and shot him with it, and then dropped it for Rachel to pick up?"

"Maybe there was a struggle," Dave said, "and he didn't have time to find it in the dark when he heard her coming. Had to get out of sight. He must have done that very quickly. I'll time it myself, but the way Zach tells it, he was down those stairs and in sight of that breezeway only seconds after he heard the shots."

"And the only person he saw was Rachel."

Dave frowned. "He saw Cricket. Celia Yamashita, the woman who runs Toyland School, says Zach knew him. Why didn't he recognize him lying there dead?"

"You just said it," Leppard answered. "Too dark. Somebody let it slip last night that Cricket was dead. Zach hadn't known. It hit him hard. He cried."

"Ms. Yamashita says he never cries," Dave said.

"Tessa told Samuels that Cricket was Zach's idol. When he grows up, he wants to play the guitar, just like Cricket."

"Another reason for Len Gruber to hate the man." Leppard grunted. "And to hate his own kid, apparently."

"Zinneman says he has a big problem with jealousy. Zinneman also says Rachel would never kill Cricket."

"So does Jordan Vickers," Leppard said. "But drugs damage brains, Dave, you know that. An addict can quit too late. You can't judge them like ordinary people."

"Have you found her yet?"

"None of the neighbors has any clue to where she'd go. She's not with her father. He's the only family she's got. Nobody at the record company where she works can even guess."

"Not a woman named Karen? She and Rachel were close."

"I don't remember any Karen," Leppard said. "Vickers says Rachel would never go back to the street crowd she ran with when she did drugs. We checked them out, anyway."

"The truth is not in them," Dave said.

"I know that, but the way they lied—nobody's seen her."

45

"Somebody has," Dave said.

"Meaning, you're going to find her for us?" Leppard said. "Your buddy Harris told Samuels this morning you're suffering from exhaustion and you need a long rest."

"And you cheered," Dave said. "Sorry, but this setback is strictly temporary, Lieutenant. I'll be fine tomorrow."

"Tomorrow, Harris wants you in the hospital."

"I'll be leaping gracefully through hoops," Dave said, "catching beach balls on my nose."

"Good—just forget about catching Rachel Klein."

He was steady again, going downstairs. He showered, shaved, climbed to the loft without gasping, without losing the strength in his legs. Pulling on fresh jeans, he smiled to himself. Those martinis of Amanda's were to blame. He'd been tired when he drank them. And they'd finished him. He'd kept going, like a cartoon character who's walked into thin air off a cliff, but it was dumb luck he'd made it to the marina to drop Callahan. It was a miracle he'd been able to talk sense to Zinneman—if he had. He wouldn't touch gin and vermouth again. He flapped into a blue gingham shirt, tucked in the tails, and the door knocker clattered.

"You have noisy neighbors," Charlie Norton said.

The music from the front building banged around the courtyard. Dave summoned her indoors. She was handsomely groomed, but big and beefy. Two friends out of the past in two days. Strange. He hadn't seen Charlie since a class reunion he'd made the mistake of going to in Pasadena back in the 1960s. He couldn't now remember why. Maybe he'd been over there on a case and stopped in out of curiosity. Jack Helmers had been there, Ray Lollard, Mel Fleisher, who'd remained his friends down the years. But of the others, Dave had recollected only a few. Among them had been Charlie, still slender then, still striking looking. She'd been wild in the years just before the war. There'd been a lot of stories about her sexual escapades. He'd forgotten the details, and so had everyone else, evidently. With her robust personality and off-kilter sense of humor, she'd won a lot of friends in school. And kept most of them, in spite of the scandals. She'd married a solid citizen—broker, banker, attorney?—had three kids. When the husband died, she grew active in service clubs, the Red Cross, Community Chest.

"This is a surprise," Dave said.

"You look fine," she said.

"So do you," Dave said. "As always. Sit down, Charlie. A drink?"

"Got any Campari?" She swept a cashmere shawl off her broad shoulders, draped it across the couch back, sat in a wing chair. "Nobody has it, but it's all I drink. No more martinis. Do they stun you? They stun me."

Dave only laughed, found the Campari, dusted off the bottle, poured her a glass, poured himself Glenlivet, and joined her by the fireplace. She took the glass and said, "I was in the neighborhood, sort of, and thought I ought to see you. You know why?"

"Because we're none of us getting any younger," Dave said. "And suddenly everyone's taken to dying."

"I reject it as the in thing to do." She tasted the drink. "But I gather it's not optional."

"So they tell me," he said.

She looked around the room. "You've had great success. What? A billionaire or something."

He made a face. "Not from my own efforts. You remember my father. He left me rich."

"I remember your father. Handsome? My God. And did he ever know it." She laughed. Her laugh had always been a treat to hear. "He made a pass at me once, when I came by your place to pick you up. Your car was bust. We were going to watch Jackie Robinson play basketball. He played everything in those days. And better than anyone else."

"Carl made a pass at you? Before he asked for your hand in marriage? I can't believe it." Dave lit a cigarette. "He was a stickler for the proprieties. If there was one thing he believed in it was marriage."

"I know. He did it a dozen times, or something, didn't he?" She laughed again. "Well, maybe you're right. But the proposal and the pass came very close together. And afterward I waited outside in the car, rain, leaky roof and all."

"A virtuous young lady," Dave said. "Too bad. If you'd married him, you'd have got very rich, and you and I could have had wonderful times together."

"Oh, I would have married you in a minute, if you'd asked me. But you chose that decorator boy—what was his name? Rod something. Dave"—she looked strict and sober—"he was terribly swishy. Everybody noticed."

"Even I," Dave said with a thin smile. "I didn't expect everybody to love him. I loved him. And he loved me, which was not as easy as you might think, you romantic, you. I have it on his authority that I am a cold-blooded son of a bitch. But he stuck it. For twenty-two years. His name was Rod Fleming. He died in 1966, and I still miss him."

"I'm sorry," she said, "I didn't mean—"

"How are your kids?"

"No longer kids. In fact, now they have kids. Harry teaches at Stanford—political science. George is in the state attorney general's office, and already campaigning for the Big Job." She wrote BIG JOB in the air with a finger. "He'll get it, too. Janice raises pedigreed dogs. I can't remember the name—the little Tibetan ones. Darling."

"You must be proud," Dave said. "You should be."

"Oh, phoo. I haven't been on Ted Koppel, I haven't been profiled in *Newsweek,* I haven't been on 'Donahue.'"

"Neither have I—not even on drag queen day," Dave said.

"Well," she laughed, "you can't have everything." She sipped her Campari, got out of her chair, went to study the bookshelves. "Speaking of the departed"—she made her tone casual, almost indifferent—"have you heard about Jack Helmers? You were close in school."

"Not as close as you." Charlie had been on the staff of the school paper when Jack was editor. They'd been sweethearts for a while. Then one of those salacious stories about Charlie had licked across the campus like a wicked, quick-moving grass fire, and she'd left the paper, and the loving couple wasn't a couple anymore. Jack never spoke her name again. And now, fifty years later, what was Charlie up to? Dave said carefully, "They're saying he's dead."

She reached up. "You seem to have all of his books."

"He used to mail them to me," Dave said.

She took a book down, pretended to browse in it. "You didn't see each other? Lunch. Theatre?"

"Not for years." Dave watched her put the book back and drop into the wing chair again. He said, "He'd write a note sometimes when he sent a new book. I'd write him back a thank-you letter. That's all. I gather that after Katherine died he took to living like a hermit."

"Gossip has it he was writing a book about all of us. When we were too young to know better."

So that was it. Dave smiled to himself, sipped his whiskey. "That would have made lively reading."

"You haven't heard anything about it?"

"Maybe he died before he could finish it," Dave said.

"Oh, I hope not," she said. "I'd love to read it—wouldn't you? Delicious. All those old backseat scandals?" Her eager smile was supposed to convince him she meant it.

He didn't believe her—not for a minute.

6

THE HALFWAY HOUSE had once been a mansion. A big frame place, it reared up with bay windows and turrets on a shacky street out Venice Boulevard toward the beach. Most of the houses were one-story cottages. Grass still grew in the front yards of a few and the shrubs were trimmed. But in front of most, the ground was bare and served as parking space for rusty cars. The mansions on the corners opposite the halfway house had torn window screens, broken porch steps, peeling paint, tar paper patches on the roof. Little brown half-naked kids played outside.

But the halfway house itself, behind its ponderous old date palms, sported new paint, new aluminum screens, neatly mowed and weeded lawns, even flower beds. Dave went up a lately laid and very carefully swept concrete footpath to the porch steps. Above these hung a carved and gilded sign: TOMORROW HOUSE. The carving wasn't good but it was earnest. Dave crossed the porch and rang a bell. A twentyish young woman in jeans, a sweatshirt with the arms cut off, and a band around her head opened the door and smiled. She was painfully thin, and missing a few teeth.

"Welcome to Tomorrow House," she said. "Come in."

"Thanks." Dave stepped into a hallway where a stately staircase climbed. To either side sliding doors stood open on large white rooms. In one of these, bulgy, threadbare thrift-shop sofas and armchairs watched a battered television set. In the other room, bare except for posters and flyers tacked to the walls and to the mantelpiece of an unused fireplace, a dozen people, most of them young, all of them scruffy, sat in a circle on metal folding chairs, talking, arguing, weeping, cursing. Dave told the girl, "I have an appointment with Jordan Vickers."

She led him down dodgy hallways past rumpled rooms crowded with beds, backpacks, piled cartons of clothing, through a kitchen where ragged young people washed dishes, peeled potatoes, kneaded bread, and finally onto a screened back porch. At one end of this were a bed, chest of drawers, bookcase. At the other end a paper-piled desk, a computer, file cabinets. The man standing behind the desk, talking into a telephone, was tall—taller than Cecil. His clothes were thrift-shop stuff, like everyone else's at Tomorrow House. Pushed back on his shaven head was a baseball cap with the lettering Boss. When he saw Dave, he gave him a quick pro forma smile, and stepped around behind the desk. Now Dave could read the message on his T-shirt. Don't Ask Me. You Are the Answer. He hung up the phone and shook Dave's hand.

"Mr. Brandstetter?" He waved at a stiff varnished chair. "Sit down, please. What can I do for you?"

Both men sat down. Dave said:

"I know what you told the police about Rachel. But you didn't say anything about Cricket Shales. He was a drug dealer, I gather he was a user." He glanced around. "Saving people from drugs is your life work, right? Didn't you know Shales?"

"Only what Rachel told me," Jordan Vickers said. "I would have helped him if I could, but it was too late then. He was already in police custody, awaiting trial." Vickers spoke with precision, shaping his phrases. "Rachel I was able to do something for."

"So I'm told. You became more than her counselor. You became her lover. You're funded in part by the county. You hold a position of trust." He pointed at a framed certificate on the wall. "Was your behavior ethical?"

Vickers shrugged coldly. "It was natural. And I don't see that it concerns you."

"She came here after finding Shales's body near her apartment," Dave said. "Asked you for advice. You advised her to go to the police. She refused." Again he looked around him. "Where did she come, exactly? To that door—the back door?"

"Yes. She didn't want to encounter anyone else. She knew where I sleep. She came to that door and knocked till I woke up."

"When had you gone to bed?" Dave said.

Vickers scowled. "What difference does it make?"

"Did you know Shales had been released from prison?"

"What? Why—yes, no. No, I didn't."

"Wasn't Rachel afraid of Cricket? Wouldn't it have been a natural thing on your part to keep tabs on him so as to protect her from meeting him again? You certainly couldn't have thought he'd help her rehabilitation."

"Mr. Brandstetter." Vickers opened both long hands above the heaped desk. "I have twenty lives to look after here. Everyone in my care gets every minute of attention I can give them. It's me and them against a world of parole, welfare, bail bonds, prosecutors, police and sheriffs, and enough red tape to wrap up the known universe. No, I didn't know Cricket Shales had been released from prison."

"When did you go to bed that night?"

Vickers sighed impatiently. "I don't remember. I've tried to train myself to quit work at midnight, no matter how much unfinished business remains. I'm getting better at it. No choice. I'll be no use to anybody if I get sick."

"When you go to bed, who takes over? Do you alert some member of your staff?"

"My only staff are people in the program. They live here. Our rule is lights out at ten," Vickers said. "No. I'm the only one up late. The telephones are back here. One is by my bed. There's also a very loud bell"—he pointed over the office door—"the kind they ring in school hallways, to wake me if someone in trouble comes to the front door."

"So there's no witness to when you went to bed."

"What do I need with a witness?" Vickers scowled. "What are you implying?"

"When did Rachel arrive? Cricket died at midnight. The little boy she kidnapped says she drove around 'a long time.' He must have said he was hungry. She stopped and bought him a chili dog and an orange soda. Then she stopped again, somewhere, and put him into the trunk of her car. She told him she had to talk to somebody. That would be you—right?"

"I don't understand about the little boy." Vickers shook his head, troubled, grim. "I thought she had herself in better control. I couldn't believe she'd go to pieces so completely. I was appalled. She threatened me with a gun."

"You weren't the first," Dave said. "When she put Zach in the trunk she showed him the gun and told him she'd kill him if he made any noise."

"Oh, no." Vickers leaned back in his chair, tilted his head up, eyes closed. The baseball cap fell off. He paid it no attention, sat forward again, face twisted in pained disbelief. "Threatened a little child?"

"Are you so sure now she didn't kill Shales?"

"She was clean, Mr. Brandstetter. Back at her job. Doing just fine. We had a beautiful relationship going between us. She's a lovely, gentle girl. God gave her a beautiful voice. I was certain with the drugs and booze behind her, she'd make a career." His face shadowed. "She'd have done it years ago if she hadn't met Cricket."

"The police are sure she killed him."

"Have they found her? Lieutenant Leppard promised to call. I want to see her. Arrange bail, get her a lawyer."

"They haven't found her. Where is she, Mr. Vickers?"

"I only know she isn't here."

Dave stood up. "Maybe here is where she'll come to." He laid his card on the desk. "If so, call me, will you? I want to see her, too. Because I don't think she did it."

Vickers rose. "I'll get someone to show you out."

"This way is fine," Dave said, pushed open the screen door, went down rickety steps, lacy at their edges with dry rot. He took a strip of cracked walk toward the driveway. This led him past a trash module. Sticking out of heaps of rubbish was a worn blue-and-white jogging shoe. He didn't think he'd ever seen one so large. He picked it up and looked for its mate. Not here. A squatty youth came out of the stable, brushing sawdust off his sweaty bare chest and arms, and blinking in the morning sun.

"Help you?" he called.

"No, thanks." Dave took the shoe away with him.

The address he had got from a phone book was of a long single-story warehouse in a sunstruck, beachside district of Santa Monica, where the only traffic seemed to be made up of seagulls and trucks. He left the Jaguar on tarmac gritty with blown sand and bleached and cracked by weather, and climbed steps to a block-long loading dock. He walked this dock, peering at signs beside or above or riveted to painted metal doors—signs for commercial photographers, advertising agencies, illustrators, magazine publishers, layout and design studios, mail-order merchandisers, TV production companies—until he found SAY WHAT? RECORDS, INC. He pushed open the heavy door and found himself in a long hallway handsomely wall-painted in bright, clean geometric shapes, and lit by fluorescent tubes suspended from studded steel rafters under a pitched metal roof. The floor of the hallway was color-coded in stripes—red, yellow, blue, green, brown, white. He blinked around him and found a directory. The blue stripe would lead him where he wanted to go. He followed it along the hallway, around several corners into other hallways. At last the blue stripe veered and climbed beside a door to a bell button. He pushed the button. A latch clicked. He stepped inside.

He had braced himself to be met by loud music, but the only music came faintly from some far-off room. This office was quiet except for the click of computer keyboard keys under the fingers of a hefty black woman whose red-framed spectacles had thin gold chains hanging from the bows and around her neck. She turned from putting green letters on a monitor, let the glasses fall to the vast shelf of her bosom, and cocked her head at him. Plainly she didn't know what to make of him. "The photographer for *Gentlemen's Quarterly* is at the other end of the building," she said.

Dave grinned. "I'm not a fashion model. My name is Dave Brandstetter." He let the ostrich-hide folder that held his license fall open for her to see. "I'm a private investigator, assisting the Los Angeles police looking into the murder of Cricket Shales."

She started to turn back to her work. "Police already been and gone."

"I'm the second wave." Dave put the license away. "It's about Rachel Klein—who works here."

"She hasn't come back," the woman said, "if that's what you mean. After what she did? She's no genius. If you know singers, especially wanna-be singers, you know they don't run to brains—but she's not an idiot."

"She had a friend on the staff here called Karen," Dave said. "Does she still work here?"

"Can't get much work done, police always bothering her."

"I don't think they did," Dave said. "I'm told somehow they missed her."

"She's in and out quite a bit."

"She was with Rachel at a bar called Shadows the night Rachel first saw Cricket," Dave said. "That's why I need to talk to her."

"That Cricket. He was nothing but trouble and misery for Rachel when he was alive. Looks like dead it's no different—like there's no end to it."

"Maybe this time she was the troublemaker. He was alive and well till he met her again."

"She never shot him," the woman scoffed. "Rachel Klein? That helpless, simple little thing? No way."

"Drugs changed her," Dave said. "Cost her her job here, didn't they?"

"Like I say—all Cricket's fault. When they locked him up, she was all right again. Men." She wagged her head grimly. "Nothing but bad news. I know. I had my share!"

Dave moved toward the hallway that was bringing the faint music. "Where do I find Karen?"

The woman picked up a telephone receiver, punched an extension number. "Karen? A Mr. Brandon here to see you. A private investigator. About Rachel." She looked Dave over. "No, lean, blond, blue-eyed. And I'd say, just offhand, could take you to lunch at 72 Market Street if you smile pretty for him. Most likely in a Mercedes." She hung up. "She'll be right out."

"It's a Jaguar," Dave said. He'd kept an old prejudice. He didn't like it for anyone to think he'd buy a German car. Or a Japanese one for that matter. "What's her last name?"

"Goddard." The woman put on the red-framed glasses again and went back to work.

And Karen Goddard appeared. Dave didn't know what he'd expected, but not this. She was tall, rangy, masculine in her walk and voice and dress. Her handshake was strong. She led him along the hallway. They passed a recording studio door with a red light glowing above it. And a moment later, at his back, came that blast of music he'd expected earlier. But it didn't last. The thick studio door thudded shut again. Karen Goddard showed Dave into an office where young women moved busily among ferns and ficus trees, working computers, answering telephones, ripping pages off whining printers, turning green for split seconds in the light of copiers. Pop music posters and album covers decorated the walls. Karen Goddard led him to an office of four desks cut off from the bigger room by metal and glass partitions. No one else was in the office. She closed the door and said:

"Sit down, Mr. Brandon. What can I do for you?"

"Lieutenant Leppard of the homicide division was here day before yesterday to ask about Rachel Klein."

She sat down and smiled faintly. "So they tell me. I was out of the office. At a meeting. Settling the details of a Triceratops concert at Universal Amphitheater. It's not important. I couldn't have told him anything."

"You could have told him one thing," Dave said. "He was here about the murder of Cricket Shales, Rachel's onetime boyfriend. And you were with Rachel the night she met him. At a club called Shadows. Maybe you introduced them."

She looked startled, and something more. But only for a second. She smiled. "You're good at your job, aren't you?"

"We'll see," Dave said. "Where is she, Ms. Goddard?"

"You think I could have told the police that, too?" She laughed. "Well, I'm sorry to disappoint you." She lit a cigarette, inhaled deeply, blew the smoke away. "She could be anyplace. If I were her, I'd be in Tierra del Fuego."

"I'll look there next," Dave said. "Do you think she was so frightened of him she shot him?"

"She believed in life," Karen Goddard said. "No—she wouldn't have shot anyone—not even that miserable Cricket."

"Am I right?" Dave lit a cigarette, happy to be in company that wouldn't frown about it. "You knew him before you took Rachel to hear him that night?"

"A long time. He was a studio musician, a backup artist. He used to work here, as he did for a lot of other record producers. I can't say I knew him—but I knew his work, and whatever his drawbacks as a human being, which turned out to be worse than those of Count Dracula, he was a gifted musician. Original. Imaginative. Terrific taste.

Then one of the engineers here mentioned he played weekends all the time at Shadows, and I went to hear him."

"And took Rachel—why?" He nodded. "That's her desk. But two other people work here with you. Why not them?"

"She was new here, seemed kind of lonely. Besides, they didn't give a damn about music. Rachel loved music."

Dave rose, stepped to the desk with Rachel Klein's name on it, and began opening and closing drawers. Karen Goddard said, "Don't you need a search warrant?"

"That's strange. I don't find any personal effects."

"What do you mean? This is her workplace."

"Women keep makeup, nail polish, that kind of thing in their desks." He turned. "I'll bet I'd find a lot of personal things in yours, if I looked. Lipstick, aspirin, chewing gum, Rolaids, cologne, God knows."

"Men do it, too," she said defensively.

"True. Did she know Cricket was out of prison?"

"She'd have told me. She thought he'd be in for years."

"Then why did she take her things?" Dave said.

Karen Goddard only stared at him. Not in fright, no. Something grimmer. But he didn't ask what. She wouldn't tell him. He said thank you and goodbye, and left.

7

A YELLOW RENTAL panel truck was parked, facing the street, in the driveway of the small stucco house in Van Nuys. A pair of trees of heaven bowed over squares of unmowed lawn. Dave pushed trailing branches aside to go up the path to the door. He pressed the bell button there, but the response came from the driveway. A voice called, "What do you want?" Dave looked. A short old man with a shock of white hair and thick, wire-rimmed glasses slid a carton into the truck and came across the grass, brushing dust from his hands. His shirtsleeves were rolled up to the elbow. His trousers were old and shapeless, the kind kept for household chores. "I'm Irwin Klein. Did you want to see me?"

Dave showed him his license and told him his name and the reason he'd come.

Klein said, "The police were already here. A black man named Leppard—a little bit like his namesake, too. And a nice Jewish boy named Samuels."

"I've heard their report," Dave said. "There's nothing in it about Rachel's whereabouts."

"She isn't here," Klein said glumly. "She wouldn't come here. It made me laugh to think the police would believe she'd come running to me when she was in trouble. Who am I to help her? Only her father, who loved her from babyhood, my only child, child of my old age, I who gave her—" He broke that off, and turned for a moment to watch a youngish, soft-looking man in T-shirt and jeans hoist another carton into the yellow truck. He called, "Did you list them all?"

"Every title, Mr. Klein," the man said wearily.

"And you numbered the carton? And the number is on the list?"

"It's on the clipboard. You want to see it?"

Klein shook his head. "Just don't miss any—that's all I ask. That Fliegel will claim he didn't get this, he didn't get that. He'll try to cheat me."

"I won't miss any." The man went back up the driveway and out of sight.

"I lost my shop," Klein said. "An Iranian bought the building and raised the rent. I was barely able to hang on as it was. Pay four times more? In that location, with robbers walking in off the street? No way."

Dave remembered now where he'd met Klein. "The bookshop on Santa Monica near Fairfax?"

"'The Shakespeare Head,'" Klein smiled. "You remember it?" He peered through those thick lenses. "Maybe you were a customer once?"

"More than once, Mr. Klein," Dave said. "It was a good shop. You moved the books here, did you?"

"To my garage." His laugh was mournful. "While I looked for another place. They're all too expensive." He opened the door of the house, gestured Dave inside. "I'm too old to start again, anyway." The living room was cool and dim. Leading the way through it, and through a dusty dining room, and into a sun-bright kitchen, he went on talking. "This city has run money mad. What do they care for books? The lives and wisdom of the best minds of the past? What does any of that mean to hustlers and gangsters? They call themselves businessmen, but they're not." He opened a refrigerator and brought out bottles of Dr. Brown's Cel-Ray Tonic. "Gouging decent people, paying off officials to get their way." He pried the caps off the squatty bottles. "Respect for literature, art, music—not unless there's a profit to be made." He took drinking glasses from a dish rack beside the sink, set them on the table of a breakfast nook. "We had a beautiful public library in this city. Downtown. You remember that library?"

Dave nodded and poured celery tonic into his glass.

"Well, do you know what happened to it? Developers wanted the land it stands on. So they hired an arsonist to burn it out. He was never caught. Shall I tell you why?" Klein drank off half his celery tonic, wiped his mouth with the back of his hand, belched. "Because the authorities were bribed to fumble the investigation. Why not? These big developers have millions to buy whatever they want—while the homeless starve and freeze, and the second largest city in America goes without a public library. It stands there, but empty. And you'll see—one of these days, it will be gone."

"You were telling me about Rachel," Dave said.

Klein blinked, frowned. "Ah, yes. Of course. Excuse me. I'm upset. Losing my shop—it's the last piece of my life I had left. First Rachel, then my wife—she died after three operations, a year in the hospital—and now my shop. Everything that meant anything to me. All gone."

"Why did you lose Rachel?"

"Because of Cricket. She brought him to meet me. He was trash. A wonderful musician, she said. His music was also trash. I knew he'd mean the end of her. I told her so. And she never came back. When her mother was dying, I went to find her." Klein winced. "I didn't know her. She looked terrible, sick, starved, she didn't talk sense—as if she'd lost her mind. She used filthy language—my little Rachel."

"It was the drugs talking," Dave said.

"She'd always loved her mother, they were friends, true friends. But, no, she wouldn't go to her. I told her her mother was begging to see her. 'Please come now,' I said, 'there's not much time left. She's slipping away from us, Rachel!'" Tears leaked from under the thick spectacles. "She ran into a bedroom and locked the door. I could hear her weeping. I knocked on the door. 'Please, Rachel, come on now, hurry.' But she wouldn't open the door. She screamed at me to go away. She was sobbing so I could hardly make out the words, but these I heard—'She wouldn't know me, anyway, Daddy,' she said. 'I'm not her Rachel anymore.'"

"Mr. Vickers tells me she's changed now."

"How changed—to shoot a man, even such a man as that, in cold blood? By you, that's changed?"

"I don't think she did it, Mr. Klein," Dave said. "And neither do you."

Klein lifted his hands and let them fall. "What do I know? I thought I knew her. Music. She loved music. The finest music." He peered at Dave through those lenses again. "You say you visited my shop. Then you know I always had classical music on the radio. Softly. In the background. It was the same at home. She was raised surrounded only by the best symphonies, concertos, chamber music. Bach, Mozart, Beethoven—the finest orchestras, the greatest conductors, never mind some of them were Nazis."

"I'm told she had a beautiful voice," Dave said.

"Rich and deep. Her high school teacher called it a huge voice. We took her to our cantor—a great singer in his time, Chaim Chernov—you've heard of him, maybe?"

Dave nodded, recalling a lieder recital, long ago, in a wooden auditorium at some Westside park. Brahms, Schubert, Mahler. A tenor like a golden bell.

"He said she should think seriously about the opera." The memory thrilled Klein. He placed his hands together in front of his mouth, his eyes bright, and said again, in an awed whisper, "The opera."

"She was working for Say What? Records when she met Cricket," Dave said. "How was that?"

"To pay rent on her own place in Los Angeles," Klein said. "Chernov retired as cantor, and left the valley for an apartment he owns there. He was her teacher, her mentor, her god—she had to be near him." His face clouded. "I should have kept her here. Her mother didn't want her to go. She knew already she was sick, sicker than she told either of us. But she smiled and let her move away because it would be best for her future. She had to study, to practice, to learn. So much. The days when a singer could simply sing, those days are gone, you know. These young artists today—they know harmony, counterpoint, what can I tell you? A dozen languages, history, dancing, acting—"

"And then she met Cricket," Dave said.

Klein scowled. "And that was the end of her."

"Jordan Vickers thinks she made a complete recovery."

"What does he know? A man who goes around with his head shaved and wearing earrings and rags? What kind of authority is he supposed to be? A onetime basketball player, Rachel said, when he brought her here to see me. What can a basketball player know? They pay them to play basketball at college—they don't have to learn anything. Half of them can't even read."

"He tried to reunite the two of you," Dave said. "Didn't that make you think well of him?"

Klein slid out of the breakfast nook. "Until she told me they were sleeping together. I don't think well of a man who would do that." He opened a door under the sink and dropped the empty bottles into a trash basket there, and closed the door. "Or a woman either." He turned and picked up the empty glasses and set them in the sink. He shook his head. "Rachel, Rachel."

Dave got out of the booth. "This apartment she took to be near her teacher. Was that where she's living now?"

"Mr. Klein?" Screen door hinges creaked. The balding young man came in from the backyard. "We haven't got a carton that will hold that whole set of Dickens. Always at least two volumes over."

65

"I'll be there in a minute," Klein said. The young man left, and Klein told Dave, "No. A young woman at the record company had an empty bedroom in her apartment, and Rachel moved in with her. They split the rent." Klein made another sour face. "Then she met Cricket and got her own place."

"Do you remember the young woman's name?"

"Karen Goddard," Klein said. "I liked her."

Before he got onto the freeway, he stopped for gas. While the tank filled, he rang Cecil from a pay telephone in a sun-hot glass half-booth beside the station office.

"Just to say I'm going home to rest now."

"Wonderful," Cecil said. "You told me you were going to do that by noon. Dave, it's almost three o'clock."

"One thing led to another," Dave said.

"And better late than never, I know. How do you feel?"

"Too good to lie down on the job."

"Since we're into clichés," Cecil said, "how about "Tomorrow is another day"?"

"I have places to go, people to see."

"What's the matter with Leppard?" Cecil said. "What's the matter with Samuels? It's their job, Dave."

"I was spun a very delicate web of lies at that record company this morning. It needs to be taken apart strand by strand. Leppard wouldn't have the patience, Samuels wouldn't have the acuity."

"Lies about what? Lies why?"

"If I knew that," Dave said, "I could rest."

"Rest anyway. You promised."

"Yes, all right," Dave grumbled.

"'And thank you for caring, Cecil,'" Cecil said.

"I hope that goes without saying," Dave said.

When he jounced down from Horseshoe Canyon trail into the tree-sheltered brick yard of his house, it was four. The adrenaline had ebbed that had kept him going from

Tomorrow House to Say What? Records to Irwin Klein's small, sad house in the Valley, and he was tired again. Too tired. As Cecil had predicted. He stepped on the brake pedal and groaned. A limousine was parked next to the house. At the wheel, a uniformed chauffeur read a magazine. The rear door opened and a stocky man with a red face climbed out. He wore a dark pin-striped suit and a homburg. The moment made Dave feel he was viewing a newscast. He parked the Jaguar, switched off the engine, and climbed wearily out.

"It's Morse, isn't it?" He walked around the car and the two men shook hands. "Morse Campbell?"

"I want to go very cautiously with this, Dave." Campbell took up the conversation as if they'd begun it yesterday and had to break it off. They hadn't. Their last conversation had been in 1941, a debating team matter. Dave almost laughed aloud. Campbell hadn't changed. He'd always done this—no hello's, how-are-you's, small talk. He'd launched right into whatever was on his mind.

"Come inside," Dave said. "Have a drink."

"I've been here since one," Campbell complained. He glanced at the chauffeur, who gave an impassive nod. Campbell took Dave's arm and urged him along into the courtyard under the oak. "Charlie Norton said you'd retired, so I figured I'd find you at home. I didn't want to talk about this on the phone." Dave unlocked the thick, glass-paned door to the front building. Campbell had been stuffy in high school. Since then, he'd been ambassador to some tiny Central American country, served in one presidential cabinet, and chaired endless futile commissions investigating who remembered what. Dave didn't think any of this was calculated to make him less stuffy. Or any brighter. He was a dimwit in school, he'd always be a dimwit.

Amanda had designed the back building of this place for relaxing in. The front one was for more formal use—except when Cecil listened to rock in it. But as Dave showed him inside, he guessed Campbell would find even this building off-putting—with its two floor levels, bare rafters, pitched roof, clerestory windows, discrete groupings of handsome furniture, looming loudspeakers, racked stereo equipment, shelves of records and tapes, large Indian baskets and jars, Doug Sawyer's tall portrait of Dave over the fireplace.

But his mind was elsewhere. Dave put him on a couch near the bar and served him up Jack Daniel's and himself a Glenlivet. When he handed the glass to him, Campbell was staring blankly with his dumb, bulging eyes at an array of painted Mexican pottery animals on the coffee table. "He's playing possum," he grunted, and tasted his drink. "He's no more dead than you or me."

"Jack Helmers?" Dave didn't sit down. He cocked his head. "You've seen him, have you?"

"I haven't." Campbell grunted, leaning forward to set his drink on the table. He blinked up at Dave. "But you have. He came by here the other day. You two had lunch together at a place called Max Romano's."

"You learned all this from Charlie?"

A headshake. "All I learned from Charlie was that you lied to her, pretended to believe he was dead. You said you hadn't seen him in donkey's years. Why did you do that?"

"It was a judgment call," Dave said. "I don't think Jack is in very good emotional shape these days. He doesn't need people climbing all over him about that book."

"Ah." Campbell almost stood up in his excitement. "Then there is a book. You admit that."

"I haven't seen it," Dave said. "He mentioned it, in passing, complained nobody wants to publish it." Dave smiled at the anxious, red-faced man. "It seems the book world yawns at fifty-year-old gossip from Pasadena."

"He did finish it, then," Campbell said. "And that's what's in it. Oh, Dave"—his frown was stormy, and he waggled his jowls—"that is very bad news."

"It's a novel, Morse, fiction. Jack will have changed the names." Dave laughed. "To protect the guilty."

"I don't know what you think's so funny," Campbell said. "You'll be in it, too. At least I wasn't—"

"Queer?" Dave said. "No. But people might find those naked footraces out on the athletic field at midnight a little strange—especially considering the trophy."

"Trophy? I—I don't know what you mean."

"Not what—who." Dave sat down. "Maisie Dwyer, wasn't it? Only she outran all of you—until the night when Chip Andrews rigged a trip wire, and the winner was—"

"Fables," Campbell spluttered. "Lies, all of it."

"And yours and Herb Forman's cutups in the Fun House at Ocean Park pier. What was the girl's name? Frances what? Hilarious, the three of you running out of there in your underpants, the night the old tinderbox caught fire. Don't tell me that's a fable. I was on the pier. I saw you."

"Oh, Christ," Campbell groaned. "And you're just reciting from memory. Jack Helmers kept that infernal notebook. Never missed a thing. He must still have it. He must have mined it for this damned novel."

"He's a recluse," Dave said. "Never goes anywhere. How did word about the book leak out?"

"Way I hear it, he phoned the Pasadena library to check up on some dates from the old *Star-News* of that time, and Libby Walker took the call, and just conversationally asked him what he was writing this time, and he told her."

Dave gave a whistle. "She'd hate that." Libby Walker had been his first lesbian friend. She'd had a lover, then, a dark, mousy little girl called Genevieve—they'd both gone on to be librarians, and had never so far as Dave knew spent a day of their lives apart. But Libby'd been pretty discreet, even in those wild high school times. And most certainly afterward. No gossip had ever gone around about the pair—not where it would do any harm.

"I'd hate it," Campbell said. "We'd all hate it."

"Oh, relax, Morse. It was fifty years ago. Everybody's entitled to act like an adolescent. Compared to today's kids we were lambs. Even if they guess who we were, readers these days aren't going to do anything but chuckle."

"That's where you're wrong. The liberals in Washington will drag me behind horses once they sniff out it's me in that book. I've given a few lefty congressmen a very bad time in my day. They're waiting out there, Dave."

"I'm sorry about that," Dave said, "but where do I figure in this? Why come to me?"

"Because you and Jack Helmers were close back then. I don't know why. Nothing queer about Jack Helmers."

"Queers have friends, just like other people," Dave said. "You're a little old to have to be told that."

"What they do or don't do was never of any interest to me." Campbell held up his glass. "You got any more of that firewater?"

Dave took and filled the glass. "Get a lawyer."

"You mean to file a restraining order, bring a lawsuit? Are you out of your mind?" Campbell accepted the glass and swallowed half the whiskey in it. "It would be on the six o'clock news coast-to-coast. No. Take him to lunch again, and ask him as friend to friend to suppress the book, forget it, destroy it." His bulging eyes peered up at Dave. "How's he fixed for money? I wouldn't want him to be out of pocket. I could see he got whatever the publishers would pay him."

"You're a fool, Morse," Dave said. "You're worrying about nothing. I told you—the publishers don't want it."

"They'd want it if they knew I was the kid took turns with Herb Forman screwing Frances Preuss in the Fun House."

"You surprise me," Dave said. "I heard Frances Preuss gave what they now so discreetly call head."

"Ho! Did you ever see the whang on Herb Forman?"

"I thought only queers were interested in such things."

Now Campbell's fat face turned really red. "Don't change the subject, damn it. Will you try to talk Jack Helmers out of releasing that book? Please?"

"All right," Dave said. "For your sake, and Libby's, and Charlie's. One of her sons is about to run for state attorney general. I'll try. But I'd rather read the book."

8

LEPPARD STOOD IN the open door of the cookshack where Dave and Cecil were drinking coffee at the big deal table. Leppard wore a summer-weight suit, pale blue, a dark blue shirt, knitted tie the color of raspberries. He looked at Dave, tilting his head. The streak of white in his close-cropped hair above one ear was bright in the morning sunlight. "How you feeling?" he said.

"Fine, thanks," Dave said. "Come in."

Cecil wiped his mouth, pushed back his chair. "Coffee?"

"Thank you." The stocky lieutenant pulled out a chair and sat down. "I interviewed Len Gruber, and he admits he knew Cricket Shales. Like you said—he jumped him one time at that bar, Shadows. Cricket had been laughing and joking with Tessa, and Len didn't like it. But he says he only got in a couple of punches before the bartender and the drummer in the combo grabbed him, and Cricket got away. He never even came close to killing him."

Cecil set a mug of steaming coffee in front of Leppard. and asked, "Corned beef hash and poached eggs?"

Leppard gave him a look of exaggerated worry. "I don't know how my stomach will handle a decent breakfast.

Eaten sitting down? Going to be a shock." He smiled. "But I can't resist. Sounds great. Thank you."

"Give me five minutes," Cecil said, took eggs from the giant icebox, cracked them carefully into water simmering in a skillet on the range.

Dave said, "And the other night?"

"He insists he told us the truth. He was in bed asleep when Cricket got shot."

"Only no one can back that up, can they? Zach was out and about. And Tessa was at work. You confirmed that?"

Testing his coffee, Leppard nodded. "We confirmed it."

Dave lit a cigarette. "What about Irwin Klein? He adored Cricket Shales. Where was Irwin Klein that night?"

"Quit cigarettes and you'll feel better," Leppard said.

At the stove, Cecil whooped and waved a fist in the air.

"Better than what?" Dave said. "If Klein knew Cricket was due to be released, why wasn't he waiting outside Rachel's apartment door to intercept him?"

"He was working in his garage, sorting books." Dave drank some coffee. "Anyone with him?"

"Alone," Leppard said. "Dave, he's a frail old man."

"Not too frail to pull a trigger," Dave said.

Cecil brought Leppard a plate heavy with crusty hash and poached eggs. The lieutenant inhaled deeply, and rubbed his hands together. "Now that is what I call a breakfast."

Dave asked, "Who was Shales's parole officer?"

"Lou Squire," Leppard said, and began to eat.

The last time he'd seen Lou Squire was 1975 up in Los Santos, where the man had transferred in the hope of escaping a growing caseload in Los Angeles. Squire had always been skin and bones. But old age had done him a favor. He'd put on some weight. He'd been pale, too, so pale as to look sick. Now there was a little flush to his cheeks. Dave had known him so long he couldn't even remember the first time they'd met. His hair was white. A good smile lit up his face when Dave walked into his office. His teeth were false, but there was nothing false about the welcome in his eyes.

"Dave Brandstetter." He stood up and held out his hand across the desk. "Good to see you. Matter of fact, you got here just in time. I'm about to retire."

Dave shook the hand. "I keep trying, myself," he said.

"You don't look old enough," Squire said. "Sit down." He started to come around the desk. "I'll get us coffee."

Dave held up a staying hand. "I'm awash with coffee. Let me ask you something about Cricket Shales."

"Now, there's a retired file," Squire said, and sat down back of the desk. "He wasn't out much longer than it took him to get down here from San Francisco, and somebody shot him. Old girlfriend, was it—Rachel Klein?"

"That's how LAPD would like it," Dave said, "but it doesn't feel right to me. The situation's complicated. Too many people had it in for him."

"They found crack in his pockets," Squire said. "He was dealing in territory somebody else regarded as theirs, and they killed him. Nothing complicated about that."

"If that was how it was, but it wasn't. They wouldn't have left marketable merchandise behind. Who knew he was getting out? Who dropped in here, or called you up to ask if he was in town, where he was living, what his plans were?"

Squire's eyebrows went up. "You know I wouldn't give out that information."

"Not to just anybody, no," Dave said. "What about somebody with official status?" Dave tilted his head. "Maybe even a friend, somebody you have occasion to work with from time to time?"

"If you mean Jordan Vickers," Squire said, "he didn't call—I called him. Yes, he's helped me out on some cases where the problem was to keep the subject off drugs."

"And he'd asked you to let him know when and if Cricket Shales showed up in town? Did he tell you why?"

"He didn't. But since Cricket was an addict, I—"

"Vickers was sleeping with Rachel Klein, and he was afraid Shales would try to reclaim her."

"He's a healer," Squire protested. "Not a killer."

"Not if he was really home in bed," Dave said.

The apartment was in one of those staunch old buildings vaguely Spanish in style, washed in pale pinks and yellows and blues, that stand in long rows on side streets below Wilshire Boulevard, thick walls, spacious rooms, tenants still affluent, mostly Jewish. The man who opened the door was forty, beginning to lose his hair, but trim and flat-bellied. He was thin-lipped, otherwise neither good looking nor ugly. No one would remember his face. Not even his mother. In some pursuits Dave knew about, this could be an asset. So could being clean-shaven, which this man was. His eyes were grey and gave nothing away. He looked at Dave coldly. "Yes?"

"Is Mr. Chernov in?" Dave had the folder that held his private investigator's license in his hand. He let it fall open for the man to read. "I'd like to see him, please?"

"He's ill," the man said. "He doesn't see visitors."

"I'm assisting the police in searching for Rachel Klein. She used to be a student of Mr. Chernov."

"She's not here," the man said, and started to close the heavy old door. Dave stepped across the threshold so he couldn't do that. "He doesn't teach anymore. You're wasting your time. Please." The man pushed at the door.

"Rachel Klein is in serious trouble," Dave said. "She had a high regard for Mr. Chernov. I thought she might have come here for his advice."

"She didn't come here." The man was irritated. "If she'd come here, I'd have known it. And I wouldn't have let her in, any more than I'm letting you in."

A voice came from behind him. "Arthur, who is there?"

Arthur was surprised and turned away for a second. It was all the time Dave needed to step past him. An old man in a shiny, motorized wheelchair sat framed in a far archway.

He wore a gray jogging suit. He was totally bald, and was struggling to pull up the hood. His movements were feeble, hands shaky. Arthur hurried to him. Dave closed the door and followed, crossing soft Persian carpets among handsome antiques and gilt-framed French Impressionist paintings, in a room dominated by a Bechstein concert grand piano.

"Maestro, you shouldn't be out here before noon," Arthur scolded. He pulled up the hood, tied its drawstring, then hurried away, his voice trailing back, querulous. "It's too cold in here in the mornings. You know that."

"Ya, ya," Chaim Chernov said. It was hard to see in this wreck of a man the straight-backed confident figure Dave remembered on the stage that long-ago night, hard to believe his labored, husky voice had once been that clear, powerful tenor. It was hard, but not impossible. There was still a vestige of command about Chaim Chernov. His blue eyes peered up at Dave as if the light was poor. "Who are you, sir?"

Dave gave his name and told his story.

"Rachel would never shoot anyone," Chernov said. "She was a gentle girl." He gave a sad little laugh. "That was not a good thing entirely for her, you know. For her career. A singer must have fire. Especially a mezzo. Carmen, Amneris."

"She oughtn't to have run," Dave said, "she oughtn't to have tried to steal the little boy. She shouldn't be hiding. Maybe you're right, but you can understand why the police think she's guilty."

"He had a nice voice himself, you know," Chernov said.

Dave squinted. "Who do you mean? Cricket?" Arthur came back with a woolen lap robe and fussily tucked it around the old man's wasted legs.

"Very sweet," Chernov nodded. Tears ran down his sunken parchment cheeks. "I hate to think of such a sweet voice stilled forever." His shaky fingers dabbed at the tears. "So young, so young."

Arthur glared at Dave. "Now see what you've done? You've upset him." He pushed Chernov's hands away and took a handkerchief from his pocket and wiped the tears himself. "Don't cry, Maestro. Everything is just fine."

"It's not I who am crying," the old man said. He looked at Dave. "It's the medication. My bloodstream these days flows with a dozen pharmaceuticals. Some of them make me cry. It's embarrassing. A grown man, weeping at the slightest thing, like a hysterical girl. Forgive me."

"Did Rachel come here the day after the shooting?" Chernov craned to see Dave again.

"What day was it?"

"Maestro," Arthur said impatiently, "it doesn't matter what day it was. Rachel Klein has never been here. Not since I've been looking after you."

"You are not here every minute." Chernov was looking into the distance. "It's a pity Viennese operetta no longer plays in this country." He wheeled himself toward the piano.

"Maestro!" Arthur yelped. "Where are you going?"

Chernov paid him no mind. He said, "Cricket had that kind of tenor, light, lyric, untroubled, pure through the whole range. Perfect pitch. A well-trained musician, too." He gave a disgusted puff. "Of course, he had developed bad vocal habits, singing cheap music. But I could have trained him out of those. And to breathe. You know, ninety percent of singing is in the breathing. See here?" He took a silver-framed photograph down from the piano. "Here they are together. She sent this to me." He passed the picture to Dave. A pair of slender youngsters, both with long blond hair, faded jeans, bulky sweaters, arms around each other, grinned at the camera. "Aren't they pretty? Wouldn't they have made a picture on the stage? And such voices—"

Dave set the photo back in place and gave him the date of the murder. "She didn't come here the next morning?"

"I tell you—" Arthur began.

"I'd like the maestro to tell me," Dave said.

The old man shook his head. "After that visit with Cricket, she never came back. She promised she would. She promised to bring him with her. She sent the photo, but . . ." The sentence trailed dolefully off, and the tears started again. "No, she did not come that day." Arthur stood behind the wheelchair and put his hands gently on the old man's shoulders.

He looked at Dave and now those wintry gray eyes almost showed emotion. They pleaded. "Leave him alone, now, will you? Just go?"

"Thank you, Maestro," Dave said.

"Goodbye," Chaim Chernov said, and Arthur wheeled him away. Dave didn't leave. He sat down and picked up an art book from a carefully polished coffee table. John Singer Sargent. He spent about twenty minutes with it, stunned as he always was by the panache of Sargent's brushwork. And then Arthur came into the room again, and Dave closed the book and laid it down. It was heavy and made a thump. Arthur jumped at the sound. "Why haven't you gone?"

"You a relative of Mr. Chernov's?" Dave said.

A headshake. "Just a friend."

"A vocal student?" Dave wondered.

"I told you he doesn't teach anymore. Anyway, I have no talent. But I've listened to great music all my life, and I love it, if it's any of your business."

Dave frowned. "You're a nurse—right?"

"Wrong. I'm exactly what I said—a friend. He doesn't need a nurse, not yet. He needs someone to look after him, clean the house, cook the meals, do the shopping, take him to the doctor, run the other errands. He needs someone who cares about him. There's nothing so pathetic as a great man past his time. You don't know what "alone" means till you've seen it. If you knew the condition I found him in here—"

"How did you happen to do that—find him, I mean?"

"I'm in real estate." Arthur took a business card from a shirt pocket and gave it to Dave. Wynn-Madden, Inc. "Arthur Madden." His hand was chilly, the handshake brief.

"Mr. Chernov is the owner of this building. I'd heard he was ill. He's eighty-five. I thought he might want to sell. They do, you know. They move to retirement communities. But he needs a large place." Arthur gestured. "You can see why—all these antiques, paintings, enormous record collection, virtually every room a museum, and so many photos, clippings, playbills from his life in music, clear back to Europe in the twenties. To give all that up for some cramped little condo among the walking dead. He couldn't bear the thought."

"Right. Does he pay you?" Madden bridled. "Certainly not."

"But it must be a full-time job. Surely it takes you away from your business."

"Money isn't everything. I couldn't bear to see him here neglected, sick, no one—and I mean not a soul—offering one bit of help, not even an hour's company, for heaven's sake. A man who'd given the world so much beauty. It broke my heart. God, how rotten the human race can be sometimes."

Dave stood up. "Not you," he said.

Madden smiled. There wasn't any warmth in it. "He appreciates it. It's very touching."

Dave moved toward the entry hall, the street door. "And that's all the reward you need?"

He opened the door. Madden was right. The apartment was cold. The sunny air outside was at least ten degrees warmer. On the doorstep he frowned.

Up the street the sun glinted on the pale hair of a man getting into a parked car. Samuels?

The car drove off. Dave turned back to Madden. "He has no relatives?"

"Killed in the Holocaust," Madden said. "Nobody left. Believe me, I've searched."

Dave smiled. "I'll just bet you have."

It was built over with expensive town houses now, but he could remember when this place was marshland. A misty morning came to mind, the silhouette of a blue heron among the reeds, poised on one stilt leg above a glassy pond. You didn't see red-winged blackbirds in LA anymore. Once they'd been thick down here swinging on the tall reeds, the air alive with their sharp calls. Dragonflies used to hover and dart, sun glistening on their wings, their glittering blue and green and red needle bodies. In autumn, fleeing the cold north, great noisy flocks of migrating ducks had swirled down out of this sky to feed. And now? Tarmacked streets curved, empty in the morning light, and very quiet. He found the address he wanted and parked the Jaguar. When he walked up the concrete strip between ground ivy to find the black door in the brown shiplap wall, he could hear the thud of surf on the beach, blocks away. He stood in a breezeway and listened for sounds of life from the handsome houses, built so close together. No morning radio talk shows, no loopy cartoon music. He laughed at himself. Children in an enclave like this? He guessed not. Upwardly mobile young couples, both working, no kids. Nobody home.

He knew she wasn't home. He had checked by phone at her office. She was at work. She'd picked up her extension and let him hear her voice before he'd hung up. All the same, he thumbed her bell push. Chimes answered. That was all. He put on his reading glasses, bent, and peered closely at the lock. From his wallet he took a sliver of metal and probed the lock with it. The lock turned, but the door didn't yield. He stood for a moment with his shoulder against the door, blinking thoughtfully. Then he went looking for a back door.

There was a back door, its lock simpler than that on the front one, but the door didn't yield either. He sighed, slid the sliver of metal back into his wallet, dropped the wallet into his pocket, folded the glasses with a click, pushed them into their case, tucked the case away. He returned to the silent, empty street, and pulled open the door of the Jaguar. But before he got inside, he paused to give the house a long, steady look. The curtains at the windows were all closed. And motionless. Someone was in there, but either that someone didn't give a damn who'd come ringing, or was too scared to risk peeping out and being seen. That would figure, if it was Rachel Klein. On the other hand, it could be a deaf cleaning woman. He wouldn't phone Leppard about it. Not just yet.

He dropped onto the seat, closed the door, started the engine. And in the side mirror he glimpsed again the man with pale hair getting into a pale car far off up the street. Samuels. This time he was sure of it. Leppard was watching over Dave again, not believing Dave would lead him to Rachel Klein, no. Just trying to protect an old has-been from his own folly. No fool like an old fool. Damn. How he hated that. He released the hand brake, and the Jaguar roared off. It wasn't young, either, but it could still go.

9

DAVE USED THE telephone back of the dark-paneled little bar at Max Romano's. He told Jeff Leppard, "When I went to see Jordan Vickers, he lied to me. He said he didn't know Cricket Shales was back in town. He knew. He'd asked Lou Squire to warn him. And Lou warned him."

"Then why didn't Vickers warn Rachel?"

"I think he did, and that's why her personal things aren't in her desk at Say What? Records. He rang her there and told her to go somewhere Cricket wouldn't find her."

"And then let her walk right into Cricket's face in the dark on her way home to her apartment at midnight?"

"You figure it out," Dave said. "You're the detective. I'm just a senile old man messing around in your case. Will you tell Samuels to stop wasting his time?"

"I don't know what you're talking about," Leppard said.

"The last time he tried to guard me," Dave reminded him, "he was shot and didn't get over it for months. I don't want that to happen again. He could be killed this time."

"Then go home and leave this case alone," Leppard said.

"Talk to Vickers," Dave said. "Find out why he lied."

He hung up and, five minutes later, walked out of the steamy, flame-sizzling, pan-clattering kitchen of Max Romano's into the sunny parking lot. A slim little Vietnamese wrapped in a long white apron followed him. Dave opened the trunk of the Jaguar and the boy bent and set a bottle in an ice bucket inside, along with Styrofoam boxes sealed shut with tape to keep in the heat. He straightened, gave Dave a little smile, a little bow, and headed back for the kitchen. He looked about twenty years old. He called himself Pow, and every time he said it, he made a fist, stuck it straight out, and giggled. Alex told Dave he was the best apprentice chef he'd ever had. He was certainly the prettiest. A flower. Smiling to himself, Dave watched him until he disappeared into the kitchen, then closed down the trunk, got into the car, and headed for Topanga.

Fifty minutes later, he found Jack Helmers's crooked, climbing dirt road. Piled in the overgrown brush next to the mailbox were twine-bound stacks of newspapers, cardboard cartons full of rumpled magazines, catalogs, fliers, big green plastic trash sacks bulging with God knew what. God knew why. After years of indifference, what had prompted Helmers suddenly to clean house? Dave parked the Jaguar in the driveway behind Helmers's grimy gray 1979 Dodge Colt. He took boxes and bottle from the trunk and carried them up the steps to the deck where cats snoozed in the sun.

The inner door was open. He rapped the aluminum screen door. The dogs came running, barking, tails waving happily. Over their racket, Dave called, "Jack? It's Dave— Dave Brandstetter." The dogs jumped at the screen. "I've brought us some lunch." But Helmers didn't answer. "Jack? You in there?" No response, no sign of the man. Dave opened the screen and with the dogs jumping around his legs made his way through the room, which was still dusty and cobwebby, but not quite so cumbered with trash as last time. He peered into Helmers's workroom. Among the tilted heaps of manuscripts, clippings, file folders, the computer monitor glowed with green words, but the writer wasn't at his desk.

The food had kept hot in the car trunk—the boxes warmed his hands and chest. The noonday heat didn't need their help. He wanted to put them down. He found a kitchen swing door, called "Jack?" again, and pushed into the room. One of the dogs was still with him. It ran around a cluttered table, and whined and nosed at something on a vinyl-tiled floor that hadn't seen a mop or even a broom in years. Dave stepped around the table. A chair had tipped on its side. Helmers had been sitting in the chair. He lay on the floor. On his side. Snoring. In a wrinkled cotton flannel plaid shirt and grubby jeans, cheeks bristly with three days' beard, he looked like a skid-row wino. But the only drink in sight was half a mug of coffee on the table. Dave set boxes and bottle on a counter and knelt beside him. The dog licked his face, anxious, whimpering. "That's all right," Dave told him. "Don't worry." He pushed the dog off, and lifted Helmers's thick wrist. The pulse beat there strong and steady. He patted Helmers's face. "Jack? Wake up, Jack." And when Helmers's eyelids fluttered, and he mumbled, "What? What? What's wrong?" Dave realized he'd been holding his breath. He'd been as alarmed as he could remember ever being in an often alarming lifetime.

"Dave?" Helmers frowned. "Where the hell did you come from?"

"I brought some lunch." Helmers's glasses lay under the table. Dave reached for them, handed them to him. "From Max Romano's. I wanted to talk to you. What's going on?"

Helmers grunted, struggling to sit up. The dog was all over him. "Would you get away, please!" he roared. "Give a man a chance, Duffy." Duffy backed off. Dave set the chair straight and helped heavy old Helmers to his feet. "What's going on"—the writer dropped onto the chair, wiped a hand down over his face—"is inspectors from the God damn fire department came up here yesterday about sunset and said they'd got a report this house was a fire hazard and made me let them in." He picked up the mug, slurped at the coffee, lit a cigarette. "Claimed they never saw anything to equal it, gave me exactly twenty-four hours to clean it up or pay a fine. You know how they are about fires up in this canyon."

"I know how the fires are," Dave said. "So do you."

"So I didn't even eat supper. I worked till I dropped. Midnight, maybe later. And I was up at sunrise, no breakfast, right back at it again." He looked at the old rectangular Hamilton on his thick wrist. "I was taking a coffee break, is all. Guess I fell asleep, didn't I?"

"You shouldn't have tried to do it yourself," Dave said. "You should have hired help."

"Nobody rents out elephants up here," Helmers said. "No, I didn't want strangers coming in, seeing how I've neglected Katherine's house."

"They didn't know her," Dave said. "They wouldn't care."

"She'd never forgive me."

"All she ever wanted was for you to do your writing. And you sure as hell haven't neglected that, have you?"

Helmers grunted. "Self-indulgence." He turned on the chair, which creaked. He raised his head, sniffed the air. "Did you say lunch? Something smells absolutely glorious."

Dave eyed him. "You sure you're all right? You don't want me to drive you to UCLA Medical Center?"

"Hell, no—thank you." Helmers stuck the cigarette in the corner of his mouth, pushed to his feet, and began to open the boxes. "I'm not sick, I just worked too hard and forgot to eat. I'm starved." He lifted plates out of the boxes and set them on the table. He shook his fingers. "Still hot," he said. "Sit down, sit down." He rattled forks from a drawer, plates from a shelf, dusted the plates with his shirtsleeve, and clacked them down on the grubby table. He sat again, stubbed out the cigarette in a full ashtray, then began pulling the foil wrappers off the plates from Max's. His eyes lit up. "Linguine with clams?" He bent to the second plate, inhaling deeply through his nose, the lenses of his glasses steaming up. "What's this?"

"Max made it with veal. Alex opts for chicken breasts. Boned, skinned, rolled in seasoned bread crumbs and Parmesan, and sautéed in butter, then baked with Swiss cheese, sliced onions, basil, oregano, and a sweet tomato sauce that was one of Max's great culinary secrets—Campbell's Soup. Nobody ever tumbled. Gourmets, restaurant critics, chefs from Europe begged him for the recipe. Max only chortled and told them he was happy they'd enjoyed their dinner."

Helmers forked a taste into his mouth, closed his eyes in bliss, and hummed. "Sure as hell beats the freezer section at Vons," he said.

Dave split the plate of linguine between them. Helmers tied into it. "This could get to be an expensive habit, Dave. Till you took me out the other day, I'd forgotten how good food can taste." He peered over the glasses slipping down his nose. "You've got to let me pay the tariff here."

"Forget it." Dave got up and fetched the champagne and a couple of spotty water tumblers from the dish rack beside the sink. "I own the place. That entitles me and my friends to all the free lunches we can eat."

Half an hour later, Dave washed up the dishes and Helmers found a clean towel in a drawer and dried them. He had been listening slack-jawed to Dave tell about his visits from Charlie Norton and Morse Campbell. "I can't believe it. They can't be serious."

"I know, it's been fifty years," Dave said, "but they're serious. Morse Campbell most of all."

"He always was a pea brain," Helmers said.

"And a lifetime of government service has only made him worse. I think when he heard from Libby about your book, Morse called somebody in intelligence—"

"To see if I was really dead?" Helmers said.

"And if not, to keep an eye on you, which they did. How else did Morse know you'd paid me a visit, had lunch with me? To Morse this meant we were still on friendly terms, which is why he came to beg me to have you quash the book."

The dishes were done. Helmers handed Dave the towel to dry his hands. Dave did this, and hung up the towel. He rolled down his sleeves and fastened the gold nugget cufflinks. These had been his father's. The nuggets were from Suiter's Mill—or that's what Carl always claimed. Dave shrugged into his jacket. "He said he'd be willing to pay you whatever the publishers offered. I think he meant more than the publishers offered. I think he meant the sky was the limit."

Helmers guffawed. "Pop-eyed stuffed shirt." He went at his heavy bear shamble out of the kitchen. Dave followed him, through a dining room still stacked—table, chairs, floor—with yellowing unopened junk mail, magazines, sealed Jiffy bags of books, decaying cartons of wastepaper. "Imagine worrying all your life that the world might find out about you running naked around the high school track at night. Get a permanent crick in your neck, looking over your shoulder."

"He wishes you hadn't kept that notebook."

"Haw." Helmers dropped into an overstuffed chair, its upholstery shredded by the claws of cats. Today, other chairs had appeared from under their mountains of junk, and were available for sitting. Dave chose the one with the fewest dry weeds in it. "He remembers that, does he?"

"It was a rumor everyone believed," Dave said.

"Maybe that's all it was. Did I ever show it to you?"

"No," Dave said, "I don't think you did."

"That's right," Helmers said, "and you were my best friend. I sure as hell didn't show it to anybody else, then, did I? Least of all to Morse Campbell."

"But you told me you were writing down in it everything anybody got up to. For your first novel."

Helmers chuckled. "Turned out to be my thirty-first, but who's counting? How much should I bleed old Morse for?"

"You wouldn't," Dave said.

"No, but it's a shame. I'd have loved to see his face when I handed him the manuscript and said sweetly, "That will cost you a hundred thousand bucks." Maybe I'll do it just for laughs. You want to set up a clandestine meeting for us—at midnight on some lonely stretch of beach?"

"It always pained him to part with money," Dave said.

"I once tried to borrow fifteen cents from him," Helmers said, "for a gallon of gas for my '28 Chevy. Jesus, you'd have thought I asked for his eye teeth."

"Did he part with the fifteen cents?" Dave said.

"You did," Helmers said. "You gave me a buck."

"New money," Dave said. "My old man was an upstart. The Campbells were old money. They knew the value of fifteen cents. Invested in blue-chip stocks, in only a few generations it could buy a whole tankful of gas."

Helmers snorted, then looked grave. "I'm sorry I worried Libby Walker, though. Before Charlie's time, she and I were soulmates for a while, both of us liking books the way we did, poetry, novels. I never said so to her, but I thought we'd get married after school. Then along came Genevieve, and Libby began not having time for me anymore."

"Did you understand why?" Dave asked.

"No. But I was sore, and when she saw that, she told me. Came right out with it. Said she didn't expect me to understand, because most people couldn't, and she didn't hold it against me. She just trusted me not to tell."

"And you didn't?" Dave said.

"If you mean, is she in the book"—Helmers shifted his bulk in the chair, frowning to himself—"I'm not going to tell you that, Dave. Forgive me, but I think that's how I'd better handle it for now. I told you, every publisher that's seen it has turned it down. Maybe it will never be printed. Why worry you?"

"Me? I'm not worried. But them—are you going to warn them if it's accepted?"

"Dave, the characters' names have been changed, the name of the town, the streets, the school, everything."

"I surmised as much," Dave said. "I even tried to calm old Morse's fears with that argument. "It's fiction," I told him. "No one will recognize you.""

"But he didn't buy it," Helmers said.

"And I think I've figured out why," Dave said.

Helmers cocked his head. "What do you mean?"

"Because your name won't be changed," Dave said.

"Oh, yes, it will. I call myself Buck Norman."

"Not on the cover," Dave said. "On the cover it will be Jack Helmers, big as life. And that's all any good investigative reporter will need to unmask the others."

"What would a reporter care?" Helmers scoffed. "Dave, I don't write bestsellers."

"There's always a first time," Dave said. "Why isn't this it? For decades, now, you've been building up a readership. You told Cecil twenty of your books are still in print. Maybe that's not a record, but we both know ninety percent of mysteries vanish like the rose."

Helmers snorted. "Dave, I'm not a celebrity."

"Maybe not, but you're a veteran writer, a hell of a lot of readers know your name, and reviewers are going to recognize an autobiographical novel when they see it. And the people who love your books are going to want to read it. And they're naturally going to be curious about who the real people are behind the names you've given them. And some magazine editor is going to sense a story in that, and then Morse is in trouble, and Charlie Norton, and Libby, too."

Helmers opened his mouth to protest, and a voice called from outside in the hot dry grasshopper buzz of the canyon afternoon. Footsteps sounded on the steps, the deck. "Mr. Helmers? What in the world's going on?"

Helmers made a face. "Goodman?" He pushed up out of his chair, started for the door. "Is that you?"

The screen door opened and a young man came in, the dogs barking, jumping happily on him, circling his feet the way they'd done to Dave. "Have you been trying to clean up here all by yourself?" He wore a short-sleeved white shirt with a tie. The jacket of his seersucker suit lay over his arm. He had a little moustache and thinning blond hair and his eyes were blue and concerned. "You shouldn't have done that. Why didn't you call me? I told you to let me know if I could be of any help, any help at all."

"No reason you should," Helmers growled. "I'm not going to sell this place, Goodman, and I can't allow you to get me into your debt and soften me up that way."

"Whether you let me put your house on the market or not," Goodman said, "I'm a neighbor. I'm young and strong. We're here on earth to help each other." He hung the jacket over a chair back, saw Dave, held out his hand. "I'm Steve Goodman." Dave rose, gave his name, shook the hand. Goodman said, "Can you talk Mr. Helmers out of being so stubborn?"

"I doubt it," Dave said.

"So proud, then? Everybody needs help, sometimes." Newspapers and magazines were still heaped high behind Dave's chair. Goodman stepped around there now, squatted, picked up a heavy armload. "We can't do everything alone."

"I wish you wouldn't," Helmers said.

Grunting with the weight he was carrying, Goodman said cheerfully, "I've got—nothing else to do—today. You sit and—enjoy your visit." He pushed out the screen door.

Dave watched Helmers gazing after him, and idly wondered who had reported his old friend to the fire department.

10

HE'D DRIVEN TOO far today. He was dog-tired again. Frowning to himself, shaking off a sinking feeling that maybe Cecil was right, and there was something seriously wrong with him, he was relieved, as the Jaguar scraped bottom, lurching down into the bricked area in front of his house, that no cars were parked there now. No glum visitors with troubles, no friendly visitors come to ease the boredom and loneliness of his retirement days. He needed to rest if he was going out tonight. And he was going out tonight. To drive back down to those town houses where the marshlands used to be. To talk to Rachel Klein. He stripped, showered, wearily climbed the steps to the sunbaked loft that smelled of pine sap. He pulled the chain to open the skylight to catch what cooling breeze there was. With aching arms, he folded back the bedspread and was asleep as soon as he dropped onto the bed.

He woke in darkness. "Cecil?" No answer. There wouldn't be. Cecil was doubling shifts tonight at the television studio. A stair step creaked. He knew the one—the fifth. Someone was sneaking up here. Heart thudding, he swung his feet to the floor, stepped softly to the pine chest, cautiously slid open a drawer, eased the SIG Sauer from under T-shirts and briefs, worked the slide to jack a bullet into the chamber. Gripping the machine in both hands, arms out stiffly, he stood at the top of the steps and said:

"Hold it right there, friend."

Below him, a gun spurted flame, a bullet whined past his ear, and plunked into a rafter. He flung himself away from the stair head, flat on the floor. He expected a second shot. There was no second shot. Instead, a voice said, "Oh, God," and hurried heels rattled down the stairs, across bare floorboards, across Navajo rugs. His would-be killer was racing for the front door. He scrambled to his feet, stood at the stair head again, aimed the SIG Sauer.

"Stop or I'll shoot," he said.

The front door opened. By some freak, the hopeless timer switch on the ground lights in the courtyard had worked tonight. The doorway glowed, but too dimly to show him more than a figure in silhouette, average height, slender, young from the way it moved. It swung around, crouched, the gun spurted flame again, another bullet stirred Dave's hair. He squeezed the trigger of the SIG Sauer. The gun kicked, the noise made his ears ring, but he'd fired too late—the door frame was empty. He heard his target running away across the courtyard under the oak. He started down the stairs. Too fast. He lost his footing, the SIG Sauer went flying. He grabbed for the rail, missed, and pitched headlong down the stairs. He had a split second in which to wonder where Samuels was. Then the darkness was inside his head.

He came to with brandy burning his throat. He coughed. His head hurt. He groaned and tried to move. He was wrapped in something. He hadn't been wrapped in anything, had he? Buck naked he'd slept, buck naked he'd fallen down the damn stairs. Amanda said, "Dave? Oh, thank God. He's awake." To prove her right, he opened his eyes. Every lamp in the room was alight. Amanda was kneeling beside him on the floor. He freed his arms from the blanket and made to sit up. She put a small hand on his chest. "Don't move."

"The paramedics are coming." It was Cliff Callahan. He loomed blond and tall and muscular behind Amanda, his blue eyes worried. "And the police. Where are you shot?"

"I'm not shot," Dave said. "Just bruised."

"We heard shots," Amanda said.

"And she came running out of here," Callahan said, "right into my arms."

"She?" Dave said, and now he did sit up. He was banged up. Nothing localized. Just everywhere. The blanket slipped down to his waist. He clutched it and tottered to his feet. And saw, seated in his desk chair, tied to his desk chair hand and foot, the manly young woman from Say What? Records—Karen Goddard. Her smooth, short-cropped hair was ruffled. Fury was in her eyes.

Dave took the brandy snifter from Amanda and walked over to Karen. "What did you want to kill me for? What harm did I ever do you?"

"I want a lawyer," she said sullenly.

"You'll need a lawyer." Dave looked at the door. Had he left it open when he came home this afternoon? He could be careless when he got so tired. "How did you get in?"

"You left a window open." She lifted her eyes to study Callahan and gave a bleak little laugh. "When I looked up and saw him, I thought, 'My God, this isn't really happening. I better get up and turn off the TV.' Only where's Icarus? Where's his helicopter?"

In the distance, police sirens sounded.

"Rachel Klein was at your house this morning," Dave said. "She saw me, is that right? And when you got home this evening she told you I'd been there?"

"You knew she was there when you left my office," Karen Goddard said bitterly. "I ought to have gotten her out sooner."

"You never should have hidden her," Dave said. "A fugitive wanted for homicide and kidnapping? You're an intelligent woman. What happened to your judgment?"

"You don't understand," she said. "She didn't do it."

"Maybe not, but she was on the scene. Why? She knew Shales was out of prison and in LA. Jordan Vickers had told her. It's the reason she asked you to hide her, right?"

Karen Goddard looked at the floor. "She didn't ask. I volunteered. Where I live now—it's a new place. Cricket wouldn't know about it. She'd be safe there."

"So why did she return to her own apartment, the one she and Shales had shared, the first place he'd look for her? At midnight, of all things. Alone?"

The police sirens grew nearer, louder.

"I never would have let her go alone. She always needs someone. She can't think for herself. She's sweet, and I love her"—tears made her eyes shine—"but she's got no sense of self-preservation. Jordan Vickers calls it a death wish. I call it innocence."

"You're both right," Dave said.

She sighed, licked tears from her upper lip, sniffed, and said shakily, "Anyway, I was asleep and she didn't wake me. She was too upset to sleep, and something she saw on late television reminded her that Cricket had hidden his gun in that apartment. She knew he'd come back for it. She was afraid of what he'd do if he got his hands on it—to her, to Jordan Vickers, to me. She was sure he still had his key. She crept out without my knowing a thing about it, and drove off to get the gun before he could find it."

"A few minutes too late," Dave said.

Karen Goddard was staring at the floor again, but she nodded. "That was the gun that killed him." She looked up. "But it wasn't Rachel who fired it. She heard the shots as she was parking her car. She—"

"And she didn't see the killer?" Dave said.

"Only the little boy. And she thought he'd get the story

wrong. She was afraid she'd get the blame. After all, she'd helped send Cricket to jail—"

Three uniformed LAPD officers came through the open door. A pair of green-clad paramedics, carrying a kit. And Jeff Leppard. He looked Dave up and down. Bruises. The blanket. "I thought you didn't need Samuels," he said.

"I said he'd get shot," Dave said, "and he would have."

Leppard tilted his head at Karen Goddard. "This the lethal lady?"

"Here's her gun." In true TV cop show tradition, Callahan handed him the weapon wrapped in a handkerchief.

Startled, Leppard looked from him to Dave. "Am I supposed to believe this man is really who he looks like?"

Dave said, "We storybook heroes all know each other. Lieutenant Jefferson Leppard, Cliff Callahan." The two men shook hands. Dave pointed upward, pain grabbing his arm. "Your lab men will find matching bullets for that revolver stuck up there in the rafters."

Leppard's eyebrows rose. "More than one?"

"Two," Dave said, and looked at Karen Goddard, as a uniform unroped her from his desk chair. "She didn't want me telling you where to find Rachel Klein."

Leppard looked at the .32. "This Klein's gun?"

"Shales's, at a guess. The one that killed him."

One of the uniforms touched Callahan's arm. "My kid sure would like your autograph. For once, I'd come home a hero."

Callahan laughed, took the cop's ballpoint pen, and scrawled his name across the back of a ticket.

Leppard asked Dave, "So where do I find Rachel Klein?"

Dave watched the cop handcuff Karen Goddard and lead her out into the night. "One seven five eight Boatwright Lane. A new development. Where the wetlands used to be."

"Thank you." Leppard started off. "I'll send a unit down there to bring her in." He dodged. "Hey!"

"Dave!" Cecil came in the door at a run and nearly bowled the stocky detective over. Cecil's eyes were wide with alarm.

"What happened?" He folded Dave in his long, lean arms. "Jesus, are you all right?"

"I slightly fell down stairs," Dave said.

"Ah, no. Dave, if you—" Cecil let the protest go, let Dave go, walked down the room, and picked something up from the floor. The SIG Sauer. He knew how to use it, had used it once, killed a man with it, to save Dave's life. He still hated guns. He sniffed the barrel and frowned. "You fired it." He looked toward the door. "Who at—that girl?"

"It was her idea." Dave hitched up the blanket. "You want to get me some clothes, please?"

The next morning, he was sore in many places. He sat on the edge of the bed and drank the coffee Cecil had left for him. Then he tottered to his feet and found he moved like a cripple, wincing at every step. All the same, he switched on music. He needed to hear music. The CD happened to be Haydn piano sonatas. Just right. Clutching the rail, he limped downstairs. There was a large black-and-blue mark on his forehead, a dull red graze along his jaw. As he faced the bathroom mirror, shaving, he was reminded of little Zach Gruber.

It was painful to climb the stairs again, to make the moves necessary to get dressed. Then, coffee mug in hand, he limped through the leaf-dappled shadow of the old oak, across the uneven brick paving to the cookshack. When he came in the door, Cecil was at the stove and at the table sat a chunky boy in a Levi's jacket with the arms torn off, and army fatigue pants. He was drinking coffee from one of the yellow mugs. His sun-streaked brown hair was pulled back in a ponytail fastened with a rubber band, and he hadn't shaved for a few days. Dave had seen him before. Where?

"You was at Tomorrow House the other morning."

Dave blinked at him. "That's right. You came out of the stable. You're the carpenter, right?"

"There's always plenty to do." The boy stood up, wiped a hand on his pants, held the hand out. Dave shook it. The boy said, "That old house is falling apart. I'm Noah."

"He built the ark," Dave said. "Is that why Vickers made you carpenter? Because of your name?"

"I had a little experience before I got on drugs. My old man was a carpenter. Time I was eleven or so, he'd take me with him on his jobs. He'd drink. I'd work."

Cecil brought coffee and filled Dave's mug. He put a light kiss on the black-and-blue mark. "How do you feel?"

"I'll live." Dave sat down. "Any phone calls?"

"No, but there will be. Soon as Amanda sees this." The *Times* lay on the table, the front page of the Calendar section. Cecil tapped a headline story with a long finger.

Dave said to Noah, "Excuse me a minute," put on his reading glasses, peered. CLIFF CALLAHAN TO MARRY WEALTHY BEVERLY HILLS DECORATOR. *Ceremony will be aboard Icarus, famous brainy helicopter.* He snatched the glasses off and looked up at Cecil. "She'll kill him," he said.

"The understanding was"—Cecil returned to the stove and loaded plates there—"the studio wasn't to know a thing about it till it was all over. I thought Callahan was smart—at least for an actor. He's done a stupid thing."

"I can't believe it," Dave said.

"Then how did they find out?" Cecil brought plates of ham and eggs and toast to the table. Noah had pulled the paper around so he could read it. He slid it aside so Cecil could put down his breakfast. He said:

"You know him?" He was awed. "He a friend of yours?"

"The bride-to-be," Dave said, "we've known for a long time. How long we'll know Callahan remains to be seen."

Noah whistled, eyes round. "Wow!" he said. "We watch that show every week at the halfway house."

Cecil sat down. "Eat it before it gets cold."

Noah pitched in. Dave looked at the paper again. "Typical. They mean to exploit it for all it's worth. Photos in every magazine the world around." He put his glasses away and picked up knife and fork. "What a circus. Cliff must have trusted somebody on the set. And old trustworthy ran straight to the publicity department."

"I hope that whoever leaked it admits it to Amanda. Because she isn't going to like it. She is not that kind of lady. Getting married in a helicopter jammed with camera crews, hovering over Universal Studios, ten thousand screaming fans milling around below? No way."

Dave smeared guava jelly on toast. "If Cliff can't convince her it wasn't his fault, I'm afraid no amount of computer magic can make that marriage happen." He felt bad about it. Pretty and bright as she was, her success had kept getting in Amanda's way when it came to men. Dave thought Callahan honestly wanted her for herself alone. He'd been pleased. "Or maybe she'll surprise us. She loves him. Maybe she'll laugh and go along with the glitz."

Noah said, "Excuse me, but what time is it?"

Cecil read his bulky black watch. "Nine thirty-five."

"Jesus." The ponytailed boy let the fork rattle onto his empty plate. "I've got to go." He stood up. "Listen, Mr. Brandstetter, why I came was—Mr. Vickers lied to you. It makes me feel rotten to say it and I been putting it off. But it's murder we're talking about here, isn't it?"

"It's murder," Dave said. "Lied to me? About what?"

"Those back steps gotta be replaced. I was outside measuring them," Noah said, "when you asked him where he was that night, and he said he was working at his desk."

"And he wasn't working at his desk?" Dave said.

"He was out all evening. Reason I know is, it was the night we have our private talk. Always. Once a week. Six thirty, right after dinner. Only when I went back there, he was going out, and he apologized and said something had come up and he had to see somebody. And we'd reschedule our conference another day, okay?" The boy looked miserable. "God, I feel like Judas or something."

"You don't know what time he came back?"

"Heard his car. I got no watch, but it was after the church clock up the street went midnight."

11

IT WOULD TAKE Cecil half an hour to drive in his blue, flame-painted van, rock music throbbing on the stereo, to the television studio over by Dodger Stadium. Dave didn't go back to bed as Cecil had asked him to. He sat in the cookshack, drinking coffee, reading the *Times*, looking often at his watch. Then he again unplugged the phones Cecil had so methodically reconnected—"I want to be able to find out how you are"—limped out, and climbed painfully into the Jaguar.

He drove south through Venice on his way to Tomorrow House. But when he passed the flat-roofed green stucco buildings of Toyland School, he slowed, peered in the side mirror, made a U-turn. He parked at the curb and got out of the car. Sounds of high-pitched little voices singing came to him. He crossed that very clean sidewalk, opened the gate in the wire-mesh fence, and doors burst open and small children came tumbling out, hopping, chirping. After them came a placidly smiling grandmotherly woman in a smock, and after her Celia Yamashita, a child clinging to her hand.

The children began climbing the jungle gym, tunneling through the barrel, piling into and out of the cars of the little engine that couldn't. Dave closed the gate carefully. The old woman looked at him, cocking her head, frowning. A question on her lips, she took a step toward him, clean white tennis shoes crunching the gravel. Then Celia Yamashita saw him and spoke to her, and she managed a smile for Dave, and turned away to look after the children, one of whom had started to wail. Celia Yamashita came to him.

"I don't see Zach Gruber," Dave said.

"His parents withdrew him," she said. "They didn't like it that I'd believed he'd been beaten at home. They said they'd find another school to send him, someplace that would treat them with respect." She blinked at Dave through her blue-rimmed glasses. Worriedly. "Who's been abusing you?"

He smiled thinly. "I have my prepared explanations, too. I fell down stairs. Will that do, or must I see the doctor?"

She wasn't in a mood for jokes. "The elderly suffer from abuse at home, too, you know. Spouses, grown children, caretakers—" Then she must have seen a warning in Dave's face, because she shut her mouth, blushed redly, and held out a hand. "I'm sorry, I didn't mean—"

"I appreciate your concern," he said stiffly, "but it wasn't anything like that." He turned away. "Where did they put Zach, do you know?"

"No, but they're feckless. I doubt they've found a place yet. He's probably at home."

"I'd like it better if he wasn't." He opened the gate.

She was with him. "So would I. See if you can make them change their minds, will you please?"

Tomorrow House would have to wait. Dave drove up into West Hollywood, parked, and hobbled into the courtyard of the brown stucco apartment complex again. No one was around. They'd set off for work a couple of hours ago, hadn't they? Those that worked. Not Len Gruber. Dave climbed to the gallery and walked along it, among the fake soccer balls and plastic tricycles, to the Grubers' door and pressed the button. The door was flimsy, and it surprised him a little not to hear the television set through it. Len should be watching his cop shows, no? He waited a beat, then thumbed the buzzer again. Nobody came. The window curtains were drawn so he couldn't look inside. Well, maybe they were out hunting for a school for Zach.

He started back along the gallery and halted. At about the spot Zach had pointed to, the spot where he'd been that night in his grimy little T-shirt and briefs when he heard the shots that had killed his idol Cricket. He studied his watch, then started, as quickly as he could manage, for the stairs, down the stairs, toward the rear patio, and to the place where Zach had stopped and seen Rachel bending over the dead man, the gun in her hand. He looked at his watch. Twenty-two seconds. He grimaced. He was crippled this morning, but even in good shape he'd not have covered the distance as quickly as Zach's anxious little legs.

Now he walked into the breezeway and stopped beside the fading chalk outline of the guitarist's body. He turned slowly, taking in everything he could see from here. He walked into the patio with the dry swimming pool. In the cool shadow of the shaggy leaning pine he turned around again, looking. A narrow walkway went out to an alley. He followed it. Cars could park here, in marked places, under the floor of second-story apartments. Rachel's apartment number was painted on the wall. She'd have come this way, then.

He went back to the chalk mark. When the killer heard her coming, where had he run to? Dave's eyes lit on the storage locker, the one Zach had found so easy to open and crawl into the other day. Dave drew out the loosened screws of the hasp, as Zach must have done, pulled open the doors. Empty. He put his head inside for a closer look. And there it was. A large blue-and-white jogging shoe.

He stretched a sore arm for it. It was stuck. Wincing at the pain, he tugged the shoe, wiggled it, and it came away. A flange of rubber sole at the heel had lodged under an upright backing board of the locker. The wearer had been in too much of a hurry to try to free it. He'd pulled his foot out of it and run away.

As Dave stood studying the shoe, turning it over in his hands, Zach piped in his mind, *There's lots of good hiding places.* There had only needed to be one, hadn't there? And close at hand. Reachable in seconds from the place where Jordan Vickers had shot Cricket Shales to keep him from meeting Rachel Klein again. While unseen by him, Rachel bent horrified above the murdered man's body, Vickers had crouched in here, heart hammering, praying for whoever it was to go away—for just the short time he'd need to make his escape.

Dave closed the locker and headed for Tomorrow House.

When the gap-toothed girl let him in the front door, it struck Dave that he'd come in vain, that Vickers would, of course, be downtown this morning, trying to help Rachel. Word of her arrest would have been on the TV news. But no—Vickers, shaved skull gleaming, was bending above the steel folding chair of one of his scruffy dependents in the big room to the left of the front hallway. The chairs stood in a ragged circle again. And seven or eight of them were occupied. But this particular child-woman, a baby in her arms, was getting all the attention. Everyone leaned toward her. And she clutched the baby as if they meant to snatch it away, and her eyes were wide and imploring. "No, no," she wept, "I won't, I promise I won't, I swear it. Never again."

"You jivin' us," a black young woman scoffed.

"Jou are lying to jourself." A breasty Latino girl blinked angry eyes. "Jou got to stop that. Ees no good."

The girl wailed, "I couldn't help myself."

"If you couldn't help yourself," Vickers said, "who could help you?"

"You," the girl cried up at him, "you have to—"

"You are the answer," Vickers said. "You, baby. You are the one that has to say, 'I don't do cocaine anymore.

Shooting up is bad for me. If I don't stop'"—he glanced across the room and saw Dave standing in the doorway—"'I'll get busted again, I'll lose my baby, I'll get AIDS, or all three.'" He patted her shoulder. "I have to go now." He freed himself from her hand that clung to his arm. "Tell her what she has to do, who she has to be, who she has to respect." He smiled gravely at them all, and came away. "I'll be back soon." He glowered down at Dave. "Mr. Brandstetter. You've been stirring up trouble for me."

"Lou Squire and I go back a long way," Dave said. "We have no secrets from each other. You and I ought to try that policy. Lies make for misunderstanding, Mr. Vickers. In this case serious misunderstandings. You weren't at your desk the night Cricket Shales was killed. Why did you tell me you were?"

"Who says I wasn't?" Vickers said. Then he noticed the gap-toothed girl watching them. "Come on," he said, and began striding off down that maze of hallways that led to the back porch. Dave did his best to keep up, halting and wincing. Vickers said, "Where I was had nothing to do with the death of Cricket Shales." He unlocked the door to his back-porch office and sleeping quarters, and pushed inside.

Dave followed him and closed the door. "The other lie—about not knowing Shales was out of prison and here in LA—that had a lot to do with it."

"All right, I knew." Vickers sat down back of his desk. The BOSS cap was perched over the telephone. He picked it up and put it on, tugging the bill down so it shadowed his eyes. "That doesn't mean I killed him."

"Maybe not, but piling up lies turns suspicion on the liar. You wanted to know when Shales walked out of prison, so you could protect Rachel Klein from him. You telephoned her at her job the minute Lou Squire gave you the news. And told her to go into hiding."

"I didn't lie to you about that," Vickers said.

Dave shrugged. "Keeping it back amounts to the same thing." He sat down. "Was it your suggestion she go to Karen Goddard's place?"

"Please." Vickers sighed grimly. "No, it was not."

"You weren't happy with the idea?"

Vickers's laugh was brief. "Karen is gay, she's in love with Rachel and always has been—hell, no, I wasn't happy, but what could I say? Rachel wouldn't have been safe here. After Cricket didn't find her at work, didn't find her at home, at her father's, he'd have headed straight here. He knew about Rachel and me. She'd written and told him."

"At your suggestion, right?"

"To make him see what he'd lost by doing drugs. It didn't work the way I thought it would. It only made him want to kill me." From outside came a shriek of rusty nails. A board clattered. Startled, Vickers looked that way. Then he turned Dave a wry smile. "I'm always believing people can be saved. That's a weakness, but I can't seem to shake it. Prison didn't change Cricket Shales, or teach him anything." Vickers's big hands lifted, dropped sadly on the desk again. "His pockets were full of crack when they found him dead. He was right back to his old ways, wasn't he?"

"Not for long," Dave said. "You were out that night. I have a witness."

"What witness?" More nails gave rusty cries. "Who?" Vickers jumped up, went to the screen door, pushed it open. "Noah—do you have to do this now? Come back later." He let the door fall shut and went back to his desk.

Dave asked him, "Where were you—following Shales around town, waiting for a chance to jump him in the dark?"

Vickers sat down with an easy smile. "I was out practicing my profession. Drug-abuse counseling. It was an emergency. I get these calls for help."

"Good. Then you have someone to back up your story."

"Sorry." Vickers shook his head. "I'm not dragging them into this. No names. I gave my word."

Dave sighed, pushed painfully to his feet. "All right. If that's the way you want it." He moved to the screen door. "But I think it's only fair to warn you, you're going to need all the help you can get." He opened the screen. The top step was missing. Flinching, he stretched to reach the lower one. "Men called before grand juries always do."

Vickers looked out the door. "You're out of your mind."

"I wish I were," Dave said, and limped away.

Dave placed the big athletic shoes on the heaps of paperwork on Leppard's desk, and Leppard blinked at them. He picked one up, peered inside. "Size fourteen?" He wrinkled his nose and put the shoe down again. "Smells wrong. Smells of garbage."

"I found it a few mornings ago in a dumpster back of Tomorrow House. The other one smells normal. That one I found this morning in an empty wooden storage locker at the apartment complex where Cricket Shales was murdered."

Leppard's brows rose. He whistled. "And they belong to Jordan Vickers, right?"

"Do you know anyone else connected to the case who wears a size-fourteen shoe?" Dave said.

"Sit down," Leppard said, and Dave sat down. Leppard said, "What kind of locker?"

"I suppose for brooms, rakes, clippers, garden hose," Dave said. "Only empty, not in use—except by Zach Gruber, the first time, and—"

Leppard nodded and held up a hand. "Ah—that locker. He crawled into it to get away from his mother. I remember it, sure." He frowned and touched the shoe again. "And this morning you found this there?"

"In a corner at the back. Stuck so I had to yank on it hard to get it loose."

"You saying he hid in there after he shot Shales?" Leppard asked. "When he heard Rachel coming?"

"That's the way it looks," Dave said. "Then got out and ran like hell once she'd gone. So the shoe was stuck—he just pulled his foot out of it and left it. Those shots had been heard. Police would be there at any minute."

Leppard's brow wrinkled. "But he was at his place, that office of his on the back porch, when Rachel came running to him in a panic about stumbling over Shales's dead body on her doorstep."

"You forget she drove around for a long time first," Dave said, "trying to figure out what to do. She bought Zach a chili dog and something to drink. He had plenty of time to get back to Tomorrow House."

"Yup." Leppard blew breath out grimly. "Damn." He looked up from scowling at the shoes. "You know, I was about ready to believe it was Karen Goddard."

"She's a regular Annie Oakley with that thirty-two," Dave said. "All she had to fire at last night was the sound of my voice. Pitch-dark in there. And she missed my head by inches. But Shales was shot at point-blank range. Anyone could have pulled the trigger. No experience necessary."

"What if her story's fake? Rachel was scared of Cricket. She didn't dare come out of hiding. She'd have told Karen about the gun. Karen would have gone to get it."

"Rachel got it," Dave said. "Rachel was there."

"That doesn't mean Karen wasn't. I've talked to Rachel—she's wacko, Dave." He tapped his head. "I can easily picture her panicking there alone in that town house, scared Karen might run into Cricket and get hurt. So she jumps in her car to try to catch up with Karen and bring her back."

"Why would Cricket want to hurt Karen?"

With a half smile, half frown, Leppard said, "You're kidding. You know the answer to that."

"Jealousy?" Dave said.

"She and Rachel were lovers. No closets for Karen. She doesn't give a damn who knows it. Told me she and Rachel were living in paradise till Cricket broke it up. They had a fight over Rachel." Leppard grinned. "I'm talking down and dirty here. Fists, eye-gouging, flying kicks. To hear her tell it, she damn near castrated him."

"No guns, though," Dave said.

"Not then. But why didn't she catch up with him walking out of Rachel's door, and grab the gun and turn it on him? After last night, I can believe that. But I've met Rachel now, and I can't see Rachel doing it."

"Glad to hear it," Dave said. "I never could."

"But we still have to hold her for the kidnapping."

"Then there's Jordan Vickers," Dave said.

"He's big enough." Leppard poked thoughtfully with a ballpoint pen at the shoes. "You told him about these?"

Dave gave a short laugh. "I still have some sense left. No, I merely asked him where he was that night. See, one of his charges came to me this morning and said Vickers lied to me earlier—he left his office that night at six-thirty, and didn't get home till after twelve."

Leppard whistled, made a note with the pen, looked at Dave. "Name of the witness?"

"Noah," Dave said. "No last name. Chunky kid with a ponytail. Does the carpentry work around the place."

"I'll talk to him." Leppard wrote the name down. "Also to Vickers. Did he offer you an alibi?"

"Claims some druggie called him in trouble," Dave said. "He went off on a mission of mercy. But he won't say who it was—even to free himself of suspicion."

"Really?" Leppard thought about that, nibbling his lower lip. "To protect some jump-in-the-grave junkie?"

"Why not?" Dave said. "After all, they're the love of his life, the street people. His reason for being."

Leppard eyed him closely. "I see," he breathed at last, and nodded. "You don't think it was one of those. You think it was somebody, with a capital S."

"The idea leaped to mind," Dave said.

"Vickers is well-known," Leppard mused, "reputed to be one of the best in his field. He's been on a Peter Jennings antidrug TV special, written up in the magazines."

"And he's in the phone book," Dave said.

Leppard made a face. "Some rock star, you think? TV sitcom kid? Athlete? Politician?"

"If," Dave said, "it was anyone at all. I prefer to think he learned from Lou Squire where Cricket Shales was staying, picked up his trail from there, followed him around until he proved he'd come back for Rachel by stopping at her apartment at midnight, tangled with him—and did him in."

"Yeah." Troubled, Leppard rubbed the back of his thick neck. "You shouldn't have moved these shoes, you know."

"Tampering with evidence?" Dave reached for the phone. "Shall I call my lawyer?"

"Abe Greenglass?" Leppard yelped. "No, please. Anything but that. No—just—just don't do it again, okay?"

12

THE WEATHER WAS changing. A hot dry wind was blowing from the east. In gusts. A Santa Ana. Blinking, hair blowing, he stood surprised for a moment on the broad expanse of white concrete in front of Parker Center, wondering where to eat. He'd asked Leppard to come with him, but Leppard wanted to be in the building when the unit he'd dispatched brought Vickers in. Dave had almost decided on corned beef and cabbage at Erin Go Bragh, where the tablecloths were gingham, the floors strewn with sawdust, and all the waiters seventy-five—a place his father had first taken him to when Dave was six, when it was already a venerable institution. He began to limp toward Fifth Street, when surprise stopped him. Across the street sat Chaim Chernov. In his wheelchair at the curb. Looking up the street. Waiting.

The light was green. Dave hobbled over to him. "Maestro Chernov," he said. "What are you doing here?"

The old singer squinted up from under the brim of a gray homburg, well brushed but bought long ago. "Who is it?"

"Dave Brandstetter. I came to see you the other day. Looking for Rachel Klein." He gestured at the sleek marble of the Hall of Justice. "Have you seen her?"

"I came to help if I could. But she has been refused bail." He snorted. "It is ridiculous." He looked up the sunstruck street. "A murder charge, they say. An intelligent person has only to look at her to know she is incapable of such a thing." He peered at Dave again. "Was it you who found her, then? I thought you were an able man."

"I found her."

"You're injured? Not by Rachel, surely not."

"She has a friend called Karen Goddard," Dave said.

The old man nodded. "I remember Karen. Rachel lived with her. They were true friends, soulmates. I think Karen would have done anything for Rachel."

"You're right," Dave said. "Last night, she tried to kill me to keep me from telling the police where Rachel was."

Chernov was aghast. "Tried to kill you?"

"With the same gun that killed Cricket," Dave said.

"Ah—so that is the reason for the murder charge." Chernov nodded gravely to himself. "The weapon. Rachel had the weapon when she went to hide at Karen's."

"That seems to be it," Dave said.

An old black Lincoln town car stopped at the curb and Arthur Madden got out. He was neatly dressed, but his forgettable face had an oddly blurred look. His voice sounded far away. "Here we are, Maestro." He bent to lift the old man from the wheelchair. Across his burden, he eyed Dave blankly. "What do you want?"

"Let me help you." Dave opened the passenger door.

He drank Bushmills at Erin Go Bragh. The basement place was crowded with men in suits, lawyers, brokers, accountants, eating, drinking, loud-voiced, making deals, making jokes, guffawing, worrying aloud about the wobbly stock market, arguing about a proposed change in the capital gains tax. Dave had a small table where his elbow was jostled by customers passing in and out, by the ancient waiters shuffling past in their long white aprons, and by somebody insistent. Dave looked up from his corned beef and cabbage. Into the red, bug-eyed face of Morse Campbell.

"You saw him," Campbell said. "What did he say?"

"Sit down," Dave said. "Have some lunch."

Campbell made an impatient face, an impatient noise, but he rattled out the old bentwood chair and sat. "I'm not here to eat. I'm here for information."

"He won't budge," Dave said.

"Didn't you tell him I'd pay?" Campbell yelped.

"Calm down," Dave said. "He doesn't need your money. Anyway, he wouldn't take a bribe. He's not that kind."

Campbell snorted. "Every man has his price."

Dave shrugged, swallowed a bite of food, and looked into those bulging eyes. "Offer him Katherine back, alive and in good health. He'll jump at that."

"Don't talk rubbish," Morse said. "Did he admit I'm in the damn book?"

"No, he didn't," Dave said. "In fact, he gently but firmly refused to tell me who was or was not in it. He said there was no point in worrying us about it, since it looks as if no one wants to publish it anyway."

Campbell groaned, caught a waiter's sleeve, and asked for Wild Turkey. "Hedging. He kept that diary."

"Maybe." Dave stopped eating and sipped his own drink. The rich peat smoke of Holy Ireland. "He gave me the idea that maybe the diary never existed—that he only put that story around to worry us sinners in our beds at night."

"And you believe him?"

"I was his best friend. I never saw it, Morse."

"Not even the outside of it?"

"Not even that." Dave shook his head and ate another forkful of lunch. It was as good as he remembered it from ages ago. Better. He'd have to bring Cecil here soon.

"Oh, he kept it, all right," Morse said, and "Ah," and "Thank you," to the waiter who tremblingly set down his drink. "He kept it, and put us and every stupid kid thing we ever bragged about into it, and now when he's ready to fall into his grave, he's going to shame us all with it."

"I asked if he'd warn you all if he got a contract."

"Yes?" Campbell gulped from his glass and leaned forward. "And what did he answer?"

"That there was no need for that, that the names of the characters, the name of the town, the school, streets, cafés, everything had been changed."

Morse gave his head a shake so his jowls jiggled. "It wouldn't help. His name would be on the cover."

Dave smiled. "Just what I told him."

"And?" Keeping his gaze fixed on Dave, Campbell swigged from his Wild Turkey again. "What did he say to that?"

"That nobody would be interested," Dave said. "He's not a celebrity, not a best-selling author. No one would care."

"Damn." Campbell finished off his drink, set the glass down with a bang, pushed back his chair. "Stubborn Swede bastard." He stood up. "Smug, self-righteous—"

"Just a minute," Dave said. "I don't know what agency you've got tailing him and me, but call them off, Morse. It's an improper use of government funds. You know that."

"Tailing?" Campbell pretended incredulity. He wasn't good at acting. It was why the high school debating team had lost so often. It must have been why he hadn't lasted as an ambassador. "You're not serious."

"I'll find out for myself, you know," Dave said.

"Nothing to find out." And abruptly Campbell turned and made for the door, bulling his way through the noisy standees. He hadn't offered to pay for his drink, had he? Dave grinned. Another example of how old money got that way.

Dave used one of three pay phones lined against a wall in a dim hallway between darkly varnished restroom doors. At the far end of the wire the phone rang for a long time before it was answered. Celia Yamashita was out of breath.

"Toyland School."

"Dave Brandstetter," he said. "I stopped by the Grubers' this morning. No one was home. Perhaps I can see Mrs. Gruber at work this afternoon. You want me to—?"

She interrupted him. "I don't think it will be any use. I think they've moved."

"What?" Dave's heart gave a bump.

"When I didn't hear from you, I tried to telephone them. The number was, as they say, no longer in service."

"He was out of work. Maybe they didn't pay the bill."

She laughed bleakly. "Mine, either, not for months. But I didn't mind. Zach needed someplace to spend his days away from those people."

"I'll make another call and get back to you," Dave said.

The other call was to Shadows. He recognized the voice of the sleek, moustachioed bartender. "No. She didn't show last night. Phone's disconnected. I think they skipped town. Mr. Zinneman's pissed off. She's into him for over a thousand bucks. Advances on her wages, right?"

"A lot of people are going to be pissed off," Dave said.

Sergeant Joey Samuels, pale and plump behind his desk, in a room full of detectives busy at desks just like it, hung up his phone, penciled himself a note on a yellow pad, and blinked up at Dave with a faint smile. "Mr. Brandstetter, sir. Sit. Have you heard the news?"

"I have news"—Dave sat down—"of my own."

Samuels nodded. "You go first."

"It looks like the Grubers have skipped town."

"Oh, boy," Samuels said. "We need that little kid."

"Put out an APB," Dave said. "Now, what's your news?"

"The bullets they dug out of your rafters last night?"

"What does the lab say?" Dave asked.

"They were fired from Cricket Shales's S&W thirty-two revolver, all right." Samuels unwrapped half a sandwich, pastrami on rye. "'Scuse me," he said, and bit into it hungrily. Mouth full, he said something to the effect that he was starving and had been trying to get to this for an hour. He chewed mightily, swallowed hard, drank Diet Pepsi from a can. "The trouble is, they don't match the bullets that killed him."

Dave stared. "How could that be?"

"The gun that Rachel Klein picked up from beside the body—it wasn't the one that shot him."

"She thought it was," Dave said.

"We all thought it was," Samuels said. "Didn't we?" He took another big bite of his sandwich. "So we can't charge her with homicide, can we, only kidnapping—which is why we need Zach Gruber."

"I can see that." Dave looked toward a glass-paneled office with Leppard's name on the door. "Where's Jeff?"

"Grilling the distinguished liar, Jordan Vickers."

Dave read his watch. "A long time."

"It's interesting," Samuels said. "And complicated. For instance, he doesn't seem to give a damn about Rachel Klein anymore."

"I figured that," Dave said, "when he wasn't down here trying to bail her out the minute the news of her arrest came on the radio. Then, at odd moments, I've been wondering if it wasn't part of a pattern that started that night, started the minute Rachel ran out of his office and drove off in a panic with little Zach in the trunk. Why did he snatch up the phone and report her to the police? The woman he's supposedly in love with. Because he's a responsible citizen as Leppard said? Or did he have another motive?"

"All he can think about is how dumb he was to leave that shoe at the scene of the crime. And then not to take its mate and bury it someplace it would never be found." Samuels licked mustard off his fingers, and picked up the other half of the sandwich. "I was sorry to have to tear myself away."

"Why did you?" Dave said.

Samuels waved at his desktop. It was strewn with files and photographs and forms. "Every few minutes there's a new homicide. How many, six, eight, since Cricket Shales stepped into the dark by that empty swimming pool."

Dave got up. "Which interrogation room?" Samuels told him.

He rapped the door at the same time he opened it and stepped inside. A tall, lean, sulky-looking Vickers slouched in a metal chair at a bare table where three other chairs were empty, except for a jacket hanging over one. Leppard's. The stocky lieutenant stood leaning against a wall, shirtsleeves rolled up, tie loosened, his arms folded across his chest. The slotted grill of an air-conditioning duct rattled faintly over his head, but the room was warm from body heat and smelled of cologne. Leppard's eyes flickered somberly over Dave, but when he didn't tell him to go away, Dave sat down. He'd begun to feel that familiar rush of awful fatigue that seemed to come now every afternoon. But he wanted to be here more than he wanted to be home resting.

"You know Dave Brandstetter," Leppard told Vickers.

"To my regret," Vickers said.

Leppard drew breath. "All right. Karen Goddard phoned you and said she'd been asleep and when she woke up Rachel was gone, and she was afraid she'd gone back to her apartment. And you were closer, would you go find her."

Dave said, "Back for what reason? Had they quarreled?"

"Those two love birds?" Vickers glanced sourly at him and away. "No, Rachel had been fretting about her clothes. She'd gone straight to Karen's from the Say What? office. Her clothes were all at her apartment."

Dave's brows went up. "Karen Goddard told us it was Cricket's gun she went for. A cop show on TV reminded her about the gun. That's how Rachel explained it to Karen."

"When Karen talked to me," Vickers said sullenly, "she said it was clothes."

Dave said, "When exactly did she talk to you?"

"Eleven-forty. The phone was ringing when I got back from seeing—my patient."

"My witness says you drove in after twelve."

"That was the second time. He must have been asleep at eleven-forty," Vickers said. "You mean Noah, don't you?"

Dave only said, "We can check Karen's phone records."

"It had to be Noah," Vickers said. "He's left us. Not a word to me, not a word to anybody, cleared off. Wrong biblical name. Should have been Judas."

"He said something to that effect," Dave answered.

Leppard said, "So you responded to Karen's alarm and rushed over to Rachel's place just in time to find two men fighting in that breezeway. You almost ran into them." He took a step and leaned on the chair back that held his jacket. He bent across the table so his face was close to Vickers's. "But you can't tell me what the killer looked like?"

"It was too dark," Vickers said.

"Two ground lights work in the swimming pool patio," Leppard said. "That backlit them, at least. Had to."

"Not enough." Vickers shook his head helplessly.

Dave said, "Try this. Close your eyes."

Vickers scowled at him, but after a second's wait, maybe only from professional curiosity, did as he was told.

Dave said, "Now, recall the emotion that you felt. The surprise, the fear, the impulse to run away—whatever it was. Get that back, and you'll see what you saw that night. It works every time."

Vickers sat still for a minute, breathing slowly, frowning in concentration. Then his long body gave a slight jerk, he grunted surprise, his frown cleared, he opened his eyes, looked awed at Dave, and told Leppard, "Mid-thirties, medium build, five foot ten, white."

"Wearing anything special?"

Vickers made a face. "I don't—yeah, flight jacket. Leather. Couldn't see the color."

"Identifying marks, beard, long hair?"

Vickers shook his head. "Plain vanilla," he said.

"You didn't try to break up the fight?" Dave said.

"The gun went off. When guns start going off, I dive for cover. Bullets don't care who they hit."

"The killer got away. How? Did he run past that locker where you were hiding?"

"I didn't hear him. When it was all silence, I started to get out. Somebody had to call the police. Then I heard footsteps coming. I was the only one around. They'd think I was the killer." He glanced at Leppard. "Isn't the black man always the killer?"

"You tell me," Leppard said.

"I stayed where I was," Vickers said glumly. "If I'd known it was Rachel, I'd have jumped out, and none of this would be happening."

"Scares me when you sleep like that," Cecil said. He stood over Dave, who sat groggily on the side of the bed. Dave hadn't switched on the lamp, but the clock's red numerals glowed. It was nine-twenty-five. "I came and spoke to you at five-thirty, at six, seven, eight. Last time, I even shook you. You were snoring. You never snore."

Dave sketched him a smile. "I'm too refined." He reached up and took Cecil's hand. "I'm sorry I worried you. I kept going too long again today. Can't break the habit."

"Try," Cecil said. "Please?" He returned the pressure of Dave's grip, let his hand go, swung back for the stairs. "Drink? Dinner?"

"I'm not hungry." Dave pushed stiffly to his feet. "I will visit the bathroom." He fumbled the red-and-white pack and his lighter from the bedside table and lit a cigarette. "You pour me a drink, please." He put on his blue corduroy robe and hobbled wincing downstairs. "And we'll see."

When he came out of the bathroom, Cecil was sitting on the couch with brandy in a large bubble glass, swirling it slowly, staring down into it, brooding. Dave picked up his whisky from under the lamp and, moving with pain, stretched out on the couch and laid his head in Cecil's lap.

"What kept you going?" Cecil said.

Dave told him all about his day. It took a long time. "Vickers denies he owns a gun."

"Wouldn't be too smart, I guess," Cecil said, "with all those druggies around there."

"Ex-druggies," Dave said, "reformed characters."

Cecil said, "What's the backslider rate—five to one?"

"You're right," Dave said, "but Leppard is going to tear up that rackety old place of his, searching for it. Because Vickers isn't smart, or he wouldn't have been so careless about those shoes. He also wouldn't have told so many lies. If he was innocent, he wouldn't have pointed the police at Rachel that night, he'd have come forward as a witness. He knew then it wasn't Rachel who killed Cricket Shales."

"Unless he's lying to protect her now."

"She doesn't need that anymore," Dave said. "Not on the murder charge. Zach and Vickers said she had the gun—that was what convinced Leppard she was the killer. But now he knows it was the wrong gun. No, Vickers was trying to direct suspicion away from himself that night, and he still is."

"What are you saying?"

"That he killed Cricket. Got that excited phone call from Karen Goddard, tore over to West Hollywood as she asked him to, met Cricket coming out of Rachel's apartment, figured Cricket was there to claim Rachel, when all he'd gone inside for was to get his gun back—"

"Which did him no good whatever," Cecil said.

Dave tasted the Scotch and breathed a scornful laugh. "'Mid-thirties, medium build, five ten, white.' Really."

"What does Len Gruber look like?" Cecil said.

"Jesus." Dave sat up, cold whisky splashing from his glass. He stared at Cecil. "How did you guess?"

"LAPD put out a bulletin on him?" Cecil asked.

"This afternoon," Dave said.

Cecil's brandy was gone. He leaned forward and set the bubble glass on the bricks of the raised hearth. "You ready to eat something now?"

"Any avocados in the cookshack? Any salsa?"

"One avocado omelette"—Cecil stood—"coming up."

13

THE HEAVY IRON knocker on the door to the rear building clattered. Dave's heart gave a lurch. Cecil made a noise, and sat up straight in bed. Gray showed above the leaf-strewn skylight. It drew a pearly outline around the young man's lean, black form. Dave put a hand on his arm, and blinked at the clock. Five-twenty. The knocker went again. Cecil scrambled off the bed, kicked into jeans.

"Those Girl Scouts get out earlier with their cookies every year." He started for the stairs.

"Be careful." Dave swung his feet to the floor and reached, flinching at the soreness in his shoulder, for the drawer that held the SIG Sauer. "Take the gun."

"No way." Cecil ran down the stairs. "Who is it?"

No one answered. The only noise from outside was the shrill wake-up chatter of birds. The steady surf sound of traffic from Laurel Canyon Boulevard far below hadn't yet begun. Dave pulled on pants and shirt, slid his feet into plimsolls, got the gun from the drawer, thrust it into his waistband, and started down the stairs himself.

The knocker went again. "Mr. Brandstetter?" The accent was Spanish. Dave knew the voice.

Cecil asked again, "Who is it, please?"

Dave said, "It's all right." He reached the stair foot, went up the room, combed back his hair with his fingers, and opened the door. He heard Cecil gasp. The man outside was compact, brown-skinned, in his middle sixties. His name was Alejandro Hernandez, and apart from the mayor, he was the most powerful politician in Los Angeles, and had been for twenty years. Yet now he was dressed like a migrant field worker. Cheap windbreaker, baseball cap, tennis shoes. He didn't smile. "Mr. Brandstetter? Al Hernandez. We have met before. May I come in?"

"Please do." Dave backed and stepped on Cecil's foot. Cecil didn't make a sound. He was too awed. He stepped aside quickly. When Hernandez had crossed the threshold, Dave introduced the two of them, and after they'd shaken hands, Cecil said, "Would you like some coffee—sir?"

Hernandez moved down the room. "Don't trouble yourself. This will be only a brief visit."

"Coffee," Cecil murmured, and went to fix it.

Hernandez stood with his back to the fireplace. Dave went to him. "Won't you sit down? When did we meet?"

"In the district attorney's office," Hernandez said indifferently. "Years ago. Ken Barker introduced us. You were making difficulties in the Rouderbusch case."

"Ah." Dave sat in one of the wing chairs. "If I hadn't made difficulties, Rouderbusch would still be locked up for a murder he didn't commit."

Hernandez hinted at a smile and nodded his head. "And now I am going to make difficulties. With the same result in mind."

"Is that so?" Dave cocked his head. "About whom?"

"Jordan Vickers," Hernandez said.

"This is really a matter for the police," Dave said. "Lieutenant Jefferson Leppard, Homicide Department, is in charge of the case."

Hernandez nodded. "Yes, that I know. The shooting death of one Howard Ronald Shales, known as Cricket to his friends—"

"If he had any friends," Dave said. "Certainly Jordan Vickers wasn't one of them."

"I have talked to Lieutenant Leppard," Hernandez said, and looked hard at Dave. "And he tells me that it is not he but you whose—understanding I must seek."

Wary Leppard, covering his ass. Dave said, "Wait a minute, Councilman. You came here incognito. You chose this hour because the usual reporters wouldn't be watching."

"This will be strictly a private conversation between the two of us. Off the record. Known to no one else."

"I wish I could guarantee that," Dave said.

Hernandez frowned. "I was told you were absolutely trustworthy. Not only by Lieutenant Leppard but by our old friend Barker."

"I appreciate it," Dave said. "That's not the point."

Hernandez narrowed his eyes. "What is the point?"

"That I'm under surveillance," Dave said. "Not in the Shales matter. It's something else, no connection. But I am being watched."

Hernandez looked sharply around him. "By whom?"

"I don't know, but since I do know who's behind it, it pretty well has to be a federal agency. They're keeping tabs on my every move, on my house, everyone who comes and goes."

"Damn." Hernandez went to the door and looked out.

"So you picked a poor time, and a poor place."

Hernandez looked at the bookcases, the watercolors, the rafters, the lofts. "Electronically?"

Dave lifted his shoulders. "Who can say?"

"Come outside." Hernandez went into the courtyard, dry oak leaves crunching under his rubber soles. He took up a place on the far side, under a clump of tall, slender eucalyptus trees. He cleared his throat, and said in a low voice, "Jordan Vickers was helping me, that night. I was the one who telephoned him. At six twenty-five P.M. He was with me until eleven fifteen."

Dave said, "You'll never convince me you have a drug problem, Councilman. I'd have to read it in the *Times.*"

"I want your pledge of confidentiality on this," Hernandez said. "I was never here. I never said this to you."

"You know I can't give you that," Dave said.

"I am in a position to return the courtesy."

"It's not necessary. If I can keep your story to myself, I will. If it means lying under oath, I won't."

"It was for my grandson," Hernandez said. "Ricardo. We have tried every sort of treatment, the best hospitals. Vickers is the only one who has ever made any difference."

"Except it doesn't last," Dave said.

Hernandez made a face. "Never for long. About the time we begin to breathe again, and feel the worst is over—"

"What happened this time? All this secrecy—it wasn't just drugs your grandson was in trouble over. What was it—a Seven-Eleven holdup, a stolen TV, a hit-and-run?"

Hernandez's Aztec face hardened in its frame of straight white hair. "You are not the man I thought you were," he said between clenched teeth. "You are a man of stone."

"What did you do—buy off the victim, the arresting officers?"

Hernandez stalked away. A moment later a car door slammed tinnily out front, a cheap little engine coughed to life, and tires shrieked angrily away down Horseshoe Canyon trail. The second most powerful politician in Los Angeles must have raided a junkyard for a car to match the clothes he'd chosen as a disguise. A rich smell of coffee drifted from the cookshack, and Dave went to get some.

That phone call of Karen Goddard's nagged him. That Vickers had been out half the night Cricket was killed made Dave wonder if she'd rung up anyone else for help. But he didn't want to bother Leppard—busy turning that monster rabbit warren of Vickers's upside down looking for a gun Dave doubted could be found—with what was only a hunch. Often over the years he'd tracked down phone calls on his own with the help of Ray Lollard. Besides, it was past time he saw his old friend face-to-face. They talked on the phone, and Ray sometimes wrote asking for contributions to prop up this or that lost cause in the field of sculpture, painting, photography. But they hadn't met for ages.

He swung the Jaguar into a white gravel driveway that curved in front of a hulking mansion on West Adams Boulevard. Big dark old deodars loomed up on broad lawns where a young man drove a noisy power mower. He was sun-browned, muscular, and shirtless. Of course. What fun would there be for Ray Lollard in looking out his stained-glass-framed bay windows at an uncomely gardener? Years ago, Ray had bought this place when it was a rat-infested wreck of a rooming house, and lovingly, lavishly restored it to its 1880s glory. He was a senior vice president with the telephone company, and owned a lot of stock. He could afford it.

Others who could afford it and who had a mission to rescue the past had restored scores of such places in this sadly rundown district in the sixties and seventies. Where had the poor people gone? Ray and friends didn't like the question, and Dave didn't ask it. But privately he figured they'd be back before much longer. Gentrification rarely stays put. The fixer-uppers had now climbed into the old hills, June Street and the like. All those pinched Gothics on narrow, high-shouldered lots, scrollwork porches, spindly towers, curved windows, etched-glass double doors. Out with the dry rot, on with the new paint. Climbing stiffly out of the car, he cringed, remembering the colors—Mexican pink, lavender, dusty rose, sunflower yellow. Shaking his head, he climbed to the porch and twisted a big brass key that jangled a bell inside.

He had known Ray Lollard for fifty years. He didn't know the young man who opened the door, blond, with a flattop haircut and an earring. He wore a houseman's coat, and in a different style was as good looking as the gardener. He had a bright defenseless smile. "Good morning," he said as if it were a treat to get to say it.

"When I phoned his office, they told me Mr. Lollard was at home," Dave said. "I'm Dave Brandstetter. Would you tell him I'm here, please?"

"He's out." The boy checked a wristwatch. "He ought to be back any minute. Do you—want to come in and wait?"

Dave stepped into the hall. "Thank you." The hall was awash in antique carousel horses, cracked lifesize painted wood carvings of Victorian children, seventeenth- and eighteenth- century signboards, nineteenth-century naïf paintings of cows in gilded frames against florid wallpaper in many shades of red. The white-coated lad led him into a parlor of buttoned plush sofas and chairs, shawl-draped tables crowded with knickknacks, Dresden shepherdesses, the silver heads of walking sticks. A bow-front cabinet was filled with tin throat-lozenge boxes and old jars and bottles of a hundred uses and bizarre colors. Yards of green velvet swooped at the windows. Layers of Oriental rugs were spongy underfoot, their colors rich and various as jewels. He kept getting startling glimpses of himself in half-hidden mirrors, small and large, down here, up there, seemingly everywhere. A spindlework harmonium gazed at him with round ivory stops. He sat on its tufted stool, pumped the pedals, played a chord. The old reeds wheezed for him. Then he heard the front door open, and went into the hallway.

With Ray on one side and the houseboy on the other, Kovaks was being helped to walk. Kovaks was a brilliantly gifted potter. He and Ray had first met at Dave's house. Dave knew him now because of his wild bush of hair—not all black anymore, shot with gray. He wouldn't have known him otherwise. He was terribly thin. The ragged T-shirt and faded jeans, worn out at the knees and back pockets, that had always been Kovaks's uniform, didn't conceal that he was scarcely more than a skeleton. His sunken black eyes saw Dave now and tried to work up a lascivious gleam, but it was no use. He forced a grin. It was like a death's head. "Hey, gorgeous," he said, "doing anything tonight?"

Ray was his old elegantly dressed self, not a hair out of place, just maybe a few pounds heavier than the last time he and Dave had met. He looked eloquently at Dave and then up the stairs, and he didn't stop moving Kovaks along. Dave stepped in front of the three men all the same, and made them halt by taking Kovaks in his arms and holding him close for a long time. Kovaks smelled of disinfectants.

He feebly returned Dave's hug with arms like sticks, and asked, "Why couldn't you have done this when I was trying like crazy to get you into the sack? We could have made beautiful music together."

"Dissonant," Dave said. "I was spoken for, remember? Doug Sawyer?" Kovaks was harking back to events long past. "Anyway—if I'd weakened, you'd never have got Ray."

"Dave," Ray said sharply, "let him go. He has to lie down. He's only not in the hospital because he raised such hell there I couldn't leave him any longer."

Dave stepped back. "Forgive me."

He watched Ray and the houseboy start upstairs with the sick man. Kovaks tried feebly, fretfully to hang back. "No, no. The carriage house. I have to work."

Ray threw Dave another hopeless glance. This time he looked to be on the edge of tears. But his voice was steady and kind when he said to Kovaks, "Next week, baby, when we've had a chance to feed you up, and you're feeling stronger." He started up the stairs again. "Come on, sweetheart. Try to walk, it will tone up your leg muscles."

Kovaks sighed, coughed, and did his best to set his feet in their threadbare canvas shoes on the steps and to climb. He wasn't wearing socks. His ankles showed dark lesions— Kaposi's sarcoma. "Next week," he said, "I could be dead. I've got work to finish, Ray, God damn it. Who the hell is going to remember me if I don't finish my work?"

"I'll remember you," Ray said to him again. "Anyway, you're not going to die. I'm not going to let you die."

"Put me back in that hospital," Kovaks said, "and I'll die, all right." A small bloodstain appeared on the seat of those ragged jeans and began to spread. "It's all they do there. Try to kill you. One less faggot, right?"

"You're home now," Ray said. "They can't get you here."

Dave turned away, went out through the open door, and stood on the porch, back turned to the hallway, waited for Ray. He didn't see the trees, the sky, the lawn-mower jockey, the passing traffic. Something was wrong with his eyes.

He knew and didn't know the young woman waiting for him when he jounced the Jaguar down off the trail into the brushy brick paved yard of the canyon place. She sat on a rock, and drew with a pencil in a big spiral-bound sketch pad on her knees. The place was picturesque, God knew, ragged, rustic. But aside from little blue-eyed Hilda Vosper, his neighbor up the road, artists hadn't swarmed to memorialize it. A white Mercedes four-door stood in the yard. He bypassed it and parked the Jaguar next to the French-windowed wall of the front building. He got out, slammed the door, and the girl stood up. She wore a big loose shirt and jeans, a little print scarf knotted at her slender throat, sandals, a straw hat whose flat crown was wrapped by another print scarf.

"Mr. Brandstetter?" She closed the sketch pad, rose and came to him. She was very pretty. "Madge Dunstan sent me."

Dave smiled and nodded. "That's where we met. You're Lauren. How could I forget?"

She laughed. "It wasn't a long meeting. Only a handshake. Zach was the center of attention right then."

Gloom had ridden home with Dave from Ray's. Her sunniness had broken through it for a moment, but it came back now. "Zach. Yes, I'm worried about him. He's gone again. His parents have taken him God knows where." He frowned. "Madge sent you for me? Why?"

She gave her head a shake. "I'm sorry. I'm not allowed to say. Madge's orders. She needs you."

His heart sank. "She's not sick."

"Oh, no. It's nothing like that." Lauren turned to the white car, opened the door, tossed the sketchbook into the rear seat. "She needs your help, your advice."

It wasn't yet noon. It sounded ridiculous, but he had to say it. "I'm tired. I was up early. I've had some very bad news. I've got to lie down." He started off toward the courtyard, the rear building, the bed on the loft. It was too abrupt. He stopped, turned back. "Look, I appreciate your coming, but I can't go with you. I'm sorry, but I simply haven't got the strength." He started away again, joints stiff and hurting. "I'll telephone Madge."

"Please come." Lauren opened the passenger door. "I'll do the driving. You can sleep on the way."

He slept on the way, all the way. Blankly. No dreams of Kovaks. Nothing. The drive had taken only half an hour, but he felt stronger and steadier when Lauren shook him gently awake. Madge came out the front door of the great blocky white house and stood waiting for him. Anxiety and more were written in her horsey, handsome face when she reached to take his hands in hers. All the same Dave said, "You're coming close to turning friendship into tyranny."

"You don't understand," she said, and drew him indoors, Lauren closing the door behind them. Dave and Madge went up the curving white staircase and along a hall where sun poured down from skylights. Madge opened a door painted with one of those swirls of color that had made her famous. The room beyond was shadowy, just faint streaks of light from shutter slats that wouldn't quite close. It was enough to show Dave a broad bed covered with the world's largest and newest patchwork quilt. Nobody's grandmother had left this behind. This was a creation of Madge's. He would have known that if he'd come across it in Cairo.

What startled him was who lay under the quilt. Little Zach Gruber. His small, pale face was battered, one eye closed, a blood-crusty cut at the corner of his swollen mouth. Dave moved to the bed. The shag-headed child didn't stir. Madge laid a hand on Dave's arm. "The doctor gave him painkillers," she said, "and something to make him sleep. He was worn out, poor little ragamuffin." She led Dave out of the room again, and softly closed the door.

"Did Len do that?" Dave said. "His father?"

"This time Zach admits it." Madge nodded. "I'm going to adopt him, Davey. It's obviously meant to be. Well, I mean, isn't it? The way fate keeps throwing us together?"

"It's a crazy idea," Dave said, "and I hope you do it."

They went into the great bright studio where long work-tables were heaped with T-squares and French curves, sketches and color renderings, gay and fanciful designs hanging and clashing on every inch of white wall. Madge pushed a tall stool at Dave and sat on one herself. "I'm his pal, somebody he can tell the horrible truth to—at last."

"How in the world did he get back here?" Dave said.

She found a gold-and-white pack on the table at her elbow and lit a long, slim cigarette. "Mr. and Mrs. de Sade drove up the coast road. Out of his one operative eye, Zach saw the seagull sign on that motel. He knew where he was. It wasn't until miles later they stopped at a filling station, and left him in the car, and he got away. He hid in the brush above the filling station till he saw them drive off, then he headed back down the highway. When he saw the seagull sign again, he cut down to the beach, just as he'd done before. He remembered what this house looked like, and he kept plodding on till he found it, poor tyke."

"Why did Len beat him this time?" Dave said.

"Because Zach didn't want to leave Los Angeles." Madge tapped ash off her cigarette. "Specifically, he didn't want to leave the Toyland School. He slipped out to try to go there and shelter with—what's her name?—Celia?"

"Yamashita," Dave said. "She would have sheltered him, too."

"But Len caught up with him and dragged him home, and that was when the beating took place. To teach him to"—her smile was wry—"respect his father."

Dave gazed across the wide room at the vast window that showed him a blue ocean, a blue sky. "He didn't say why Len decided so suddenly to clear out."

"No. Will he have to testify against Rachel Klein?"

"Not for murder. The gun Zach saw her pick up from beside the victim's body wasn't the gun that killed Shales."

"So she's not being charged with homicide?"

"Only child-stealing, flight to avoid prosecution, concealing evidence, little stuff like that. But Shales is still dead, and somebody shot him."

"Len Gruber?" Madge asked. "You think he saw the story on the television news, and that was why he ran away?"

"No." Dave had been trying to skip smoking. But now he took one of Madge's cigarettes and lit it with her lighter. "He'd already left by the time the story broke."

Madge frowned. "Then his reason doesn't connect?"

"It connects. How? Try this. As long as Rachel wasn't caught, he had nothing to fear. But once they caught her, he knew it would be only a matter of hours till they learned the gun she had with her wasn't the murder weapon."

"Ah. That's why they didn't stay at that filling station until they'd found Zach. They were in a panic to put distance between themselves and the police."

"Something like that," Dave said.

"Why would Len Gruber have wanted to kill this Shales boy? Were they enemies?"

"They weren't friends." Dave told Madge about the fight over Tessa at Shadows. "When we first interviewed Gruber, he denied he knew Shales. That kind of lie doesn't sit well with the police. Or with me. Still, I find it hard to believe he'd kill Cricket just for prowling around that apartment complex—when Tessa wasn't even there."

"But why run away, then?" Madge said. "Doesn't that look bad to the police, too? Doesn't that shout guilt?"

"The Grubers aren't gifted with brains." Dave smoked in grim silence for a minute. Then he said, "Maybe he was out that night looking for Zach—I've suspected that all along. And he saw the shooting and knows who killed Cricket and is afraid to be a witness for fear he'll end up dead himself."

Madge put out her cigarette. "Or maybe when they catch up to him, the police will find a gun in the car. The gun that did the killing."

"Unless he's thrown it into the ocean." Dave sighed.

Madge smiled and slid off the stool. "Come have some lunch," she said. "Lauren makes the most elegant—"

Dave missed his footing, getting off the stool. Madge caught his arm. "Are you all right? I'm worried about you, Davey. You're looking so—frail, lately."

14

THEY LAY IN bed on the dark sleeping loft. The Santa Ana wind had come back. Dave had forgotten, and left the skylight open all day. Bed, stereo equipment, television set, chest of drawers, braided rugs, everything had gotten strewn with dry leaves, twigs, seed pods, pine needles. And a gritty film of dust. Cecil, home from work while Dave napped exhausted at Madge's, had vacuumed it up. But it didn't stop. At every house-shaking gust, more of it pattered down. It was hot. The skylight had to be open, so there was nothing to do but ignore it. They ignored it.

"Ray never said a word to me," Dave said. "Or to anyone else, it seems. Madge hadn't heard."

"Explains why they dodged the reopening at Max's," Cecil said. "Why he kept making excuses for the two of them not coming over here the way they used to."

"Mmm." Dave lay quiet for a time. "Kovaks was such a wild one. You never knew what he'd do next. He never knew."

"It incubates a long, evil time—years," Cecil said. "Lurks there in the bloodstream, waiting, and you never know. When was it he and Ray started living together?"

"Longer ago than that," Dave said. "Before AIDS was ever heard of."

"So they weren't monogamous," Cecil said.

"There were those so-called shop assistants." Dave sighed and turned on his side. "Monogamy is what Ray would have wanted. I know Ray. But could he control Kovaks? Could Kovaks? In a time when not even the sanest of us guessed sex with beautiful strangers could cost us our lives?"

Cecil said, "Sex with beautiful strangers? You, Dave?"

Dave switched to his left side, pushed himself up on his elbow, looked down at the dark elegant shape of Cecil's head on the white pillow. He was grinning. His teeth showed. Dave said, "You were a beautiful stranger."

"So were you," Cecil said, and raised his head and kissed him. He ran a wistful hand down Dave's arm. "Seems lately like you're becoming that again."

Dave frowned. "What's this?"

"A stranger," Cecil said. "Come on, admit it—we don't do a lot of loving anymore, now do we?"

"If it was every day"—it was Dave's turn to do the kissing— "it wouldn't be enough for me."

"In your mind." Cecil laughed. "I know. I can see it in your eyes when you look at me. I'm as narcissistic as the next faggot. I love it. I preen." The laughter left his voice. He put his arms around Dave and drew him against his nakedness. "But with so many dying"—his breath was warm in Dave's ear, his voice shaky—"we better love each other for real, and all we can—we're so lucky to have the chance."

The wind had swept the sky clear. The hills stood out sharply as he drove the San Diego Freeway through the pass to the Valley. It was the kind of morning that made him despair. It would draw a hundred thousand new settlers before the week was out. California already had more people than Norway, Sweden, Denmark put together. With weather like this, soon the whole damn country would be moving in. He laughed at himself. What the hell difference did it make now? He'd never live to see it.

He pushed a CD into the dash. Ashkenazy played Mozart. And by the time he reached his off-ramp, he was at peace with the world. Almost.

When he pulled up in front of the Klein house, Irwin Klein was using clippers on the trailing branches of one of the two trees of heaven in the front. His shirt was sweaty. Leafy loppings lay around his feet. He stopped his work and stared at Dave through those thick lenses of his. Dave got out of the Jaguar and walked to him.

"Good morning, Mr. Klein."

"Mr. Brandstetter? What brings you here? I'm cleaning up the place. The sand blasters will be here tomorrow. After that the exterior painters. Already, inside they—"

"This looks like hard work," Dave said. "Couldn't you get a kid from the neighborhood?"

Klein made a face and turned for the house, waving a hand. "You're thinking of another day and age. Kids from the neighborhood don't work for quarters anymore. They want the minimum wage. They want a contract with fringe benefits—Social Security, sick pay, a free trip to Hawaii every summer." He dropped the clippers, opened the screen door. "Come in. It's time for a coffee break."

Dave stepped into the sad gray living room. "You're going to sell the house?"

"Why not? Why fool myself?" Klein led the way through the dining room. "Is my life just beginning? Does the future lie golden before me? Who needs all these rooms? At my age, the law will let me keep the money tax-free and live off it." He pushed the kitchen swing door. There was a smell of fresh paint. "A bachelor flat will do for me."

"This looks very nice," Dave said.

"Paint on an old wall works better than paint on an old woman." Klein got mugs from a cupboard, spooned instant coffee from a jar, poured in water from a kettle on the stove. From the refrigerator he got a small carton of half-and-half. He set this on the table in the breakfast nook. "It only makes a woman look older. It makes a room look brand new." He set the mugs on the table. "Sit down, Mr. Brandstetter. What brings you back to me?"

"You had holdups at your shop." Dave sat down.

"Only one, but it was enough, thank you. *Schvartzahs.* Panicky street boys. As out of place in a bookstore as rats at a banquet." He fetched spoons, then sat down himself, across from Dave. "The minute the bell gave its little jingle and I looked up and saw them"—he poured cream into his coffee and stirred it—"I knew what they'd come for."

"Did they get much?" Dave asked.

Klein waved a small hand. The handles of the clippers had left blisters on his palm. "Who's counting? They didn't kill me, didn't turn me into a vegetable." He laughed ruefully. "They frightened me, I admit it. It was hours before I stopped shaking. They also made me very angry." He drank some of his coffee. "It's so—demeaning to the dignity. Invaded, raped. By the new barbarians. Sacked."

"They vandalized the store?"

"No, no. All they wanted was the money, for drugs, I suppose. They ran as soon as they had it. But I felt so—so—outraged. And the police?" He rolled his eyes behind their distorting lenses. "They acted =as if it were the most ordinary event. It was a half hour before they strolled in. And they didn't bother to conceal how boring was my little robbery, my loss of a few hundred dollars." He shook his head and sipped his coffee again. "And would I ever get it back? They doubted it. They advised me not to keep the shop open at night." He snorted disgust. "So now they're business experts? My best trade was at night."

"And so you bought a gun," Dave said. "A thirty-two caliber revolver—isn't that right?" Klein paled. He stared. He worked his mouth but no words came. He gulped from his mug and the coffee went down the wrong way. He had a coughing fit. Gasping, he finally said, "No. What gave you such an idea?" He slid out of the breakfast nook to find a box of tissues on a counter, and dry his eyes. He put the glasses back on and sat at the table again.

"A gun? I have a horror of guns."

"So have I," Dave said. "But I own one."

Klein gave a couple of small residual coughs, drank again, and said, "What made you think such a thing?"

"After they've been held up," Dave said, "shopkeepers often decide to buy guns."

"Someone said, 'Buy a dog. *Schvartzahs* are deathly afraid of dogs.'" Klein smiled wanly. "But so am I."

Dave tried the coffee. It was unspeakable. "Have you heard the good news?" he said. "The district attorney has dropped the murder charge against Rachel."

"Ah." Klein's face lit up. "That's wonderful. Of course, I knew she would never do such a thing, but what others would do—police and law courts—who can say? It would not be the first time an innocent—" He tilted his head, warily. "Why? Why did they drop the murder charge?"

"Because the gun she had wasn't the one that killed Shales," Dave said. Klein said nothing, he simply stared. "When Jordan Vickers telephoned Rachel at her workplace to warn her Shales was out of prison and in Los Angeles, she left the record company right away, and went into hiding at Karen Goddard's apartment—a town house near the marina. Later, she remembered that Shales had left his gun hidden at her apartment before he went to jail. She was afraid if he got it again, he'd use it on her, or on Vickers, or Karen. So in the middle of the night, when Karen was asleep, Rachel drove to West LA to try to get the gun before he could get it. And you know what happened after that."

"The police told me," Klein said. "The television."

"Not the whole story, though, did they?" Dave said. "You know more about it than they do."

"I? I?" Klein sat back sharply, laid a hand on his chest. "What are you talking about?"

"Telephone company records," Dave said, "show that Karen Goddard telephoned you that night at seventeen minutes past eleven." Klein grew red in the face, and started to deny it, and Dave held up a hand. "Don't tell me you were in the garage sorting books and didn't hear the phone ring. You took the call. It lasted almost four minutes."

Klein seemed to shrink in his place. At last, he raised his brows, blew out air, opened his hands. "What can I say? She called. She was frantic that Rachel would go there and run into Cricket. She said she'd been trying to reach Vickers but no one answered. She begged me to go head Rachel off, protect her, do whatever I could."

"And she's your daughter, and no matter how she's hurt you, you love her. So you went. And took your gun along."

"I'm an old man," Klein said. "Cricket Shales is not the Incredible Hulk, but he's young and strong. Yes, I took the gun—what did you expect?"

"That's what I expected." Dave smiled and slid out of the booth. "You want to show it to me, please?"

"What?" Klein goggled up at him. "Why, no, that is—"

"You haven't got it—is that what you're saying?"

"I haven't got it." He stared at his hands. His voice was small. "I'm no Rambo. It was dark in those patios. I took out the gun and tiptoed toward Rachel's apartment. I was trembling, I was sure Cricket would jump out at me at any minute. Instead"—he laughed dolefully—"someone crept up behind me, put an arm around my throat, and choked me till I lost consciousness. When I woke I was lying on my face on cement and the gun was gone. All I could think of was Rachel. I started for her door, and here was Cricket lying dead. I heard sirens. The police were coming. I was sure it was my gun that had shot him. I was afraid they'd arrest me. I ran—past the swimming pool and out the back."

Something was going to have to be done. When Dave pulled open the heavy front door of Max Romano's to usher Jeff Leppard inside, eleven people stood waiting to be seated, and all the tables were occupied. The small dark bar was crowded, too—and some of the drinkers would be wanting lunch as well.

"Business," he grunted to Leppard, as they edged their way through the hopeful, "is getting too damn good."

He led the way to his table in its far shadowy corner under a stained-glass window and felt guilty about it. Was he going to have to give up the privilege of always having his own table, which he'd bought the place to keep? Not that the table was the whole story. He'd bought Max's to hang on to a thousand memories. And to keep the present from vanishing into the past. The place was filled with the ghosts of people he'd loved and lost. Until he joined them in oblivion, he wanted to keep remembering them here.

"You could refuse service to coloreds," Leppard said.

"Or Scandinavians," Dave said.

When Leppard's white wine and Dave's Dos Equis had come, Leppard said, "We checked out what you said on the phone. It's a Colt, registered in 1976 to a Herschel Klein, all right. Irwin's brother. Kosher butcher. When he died in 1981, the widow didn't know what to do with it, so she kept it. When Irwin told her about the robbery, she said, 'Take it, the police won't protect you, protect yourself.'"

"And he took it"—Dave lit a cigarette—"and now he wishes he hadn't."

"That sounded like a combat move," Leppard said, "the arm around the throat from behind."

"Is Len Gruber a veteran?" Dave said.

"No record of it," Leppard said. "But we've been assembling another kind of record from around the country."

"Brawling?" Dave took warm bread from a basket and buttered it. "Is that why he can't hold a job? 'Around the country'? Is that why he has to keep moving on?"

"You got it," Leppard said. "He was here in LA almost five years, because it's big, but mostly because they liked Tessa at Shadows." Leppard nibbled his salad. "After what he did to Zach this time, I hope we find the son of a bitch."

"I hope you find Irwin Klein's gun in his glove compartment," Dave said, "but I doubt it. Unless you can also find there a better motive for him to kill Cricket than jealousy."

"Same as Jordan Vickers's," Leppard said. "Motive is not something we've really got much of in this case."

Dave blinked at him. "Not so far. None of it seems to me to add up. Who really cared enough whether Cricket Shales lived or died to take the risk of killing him?"

Leppard smiled sourly. "Not much of a risk to date," he said. "We're a long way from catching them, whoever they are. I really liked Karen Goddard for it. But you ruined that with your telephone company research." He looked at Dave sharply. "Just how did you manage that?"

"When you've been in this business as long as I have—"

"Spare me how cold it was living in those caves."

"—you'll understand there's nothing secret in this world as long as one living person knows it."

"We have access to those records," Leppard said. "No one else except the subscriber himself is supposed to."

Dave said, "Only you didn't get around to using your legal right, and I did get around to using my shady one."

"And we lose Karen Goddard as a suspect." Leppard hungrily watched the waiter set down a tray on its folding stand and lay plates on the table, murmuring cautions about how hot they were.

"But we gain a line on the missing gun," Dave said. "Not on where it is, or on who used it—if anybody used it. We sure as hell didn't find it at Tomorrow House."

Leppard inhaled steam from his lasagna and sighed with delight. "Damn shame. Vickers was at the apartment complex when Shales was killed." Leppard picked up his fork and began to eat. "He could easily have put Klein's lights out and commandeered his gun."

"If any of that really happened. It could be a lie." Dave laid open his sand dabs and lifted out the fragile skeletons. "Klein could have shot Cricket himself."

"Vickers said the killer was in his thirties."

"Vickers said a lot of things," Dave said. "If it turns out Len Gruber has the gun, then he's Plain Vanilla. And I take back my distrust of Vickers. If not—"

A big figure loomed at the table. Dave looked up. It was Cliff Callahan. His face was anguished. He gave Leppard a nod. "Lieutenant?" He sat down and said to Dave, "I'm sorry to intrude, but I'm in deep trouble."

"About that whirlybird wedding?" Dave said.

"You've got it. Amanda isn't speaking to me. She's really boiled. And I didn't do it, Dave. I swear."

"Then how did the studio publicity department find out? You and Amanda, Cecil and I were the only people who knew, and it wasn't me."

"What about Cecil?" Callahan said. "He's a reporter."

Dave said, "He'd never violate a personal confidence."

"No," Callahan said sheepishly. "I didn't think so."

"I never saw your names linked in the paper, or on television. You didn't go to Beverly Hills parties or charity balls together. But you did go out now and then, didn't you—restaurants, theatres, movies? And you're too big to hide behind a pair of dark glasses."

"Sure, we went out, but not to celebrity places."

"Anyplace a celebrity goes is a celebrity place," Dave said. "Some freelance reporter scented a romance, and began keeping an eye on the two of you. When you came breezing out of the Hall of Records, a quick word with the clerk would have been all they needed."

Callahan's bulky muscles relaxed a little. He ventured a hopeful smile. "Will you please tell that to Amanda?"

"If you're going to be married," Dave said, "it seems to me she ought to learn to take your word for these things."

"We're still new to each other," Callahan said. "I don't blame her for not wanting to make a clown act out of her wedding—our wedding. I just wish she'd stop thinking because I'm an actor I'd trash her feelings just to satisfy my stupid ego. It's not true, damn it."

"She worries about making a mistake," Dave said. "She's almost done that more than once. Don't take it personally."

"You'll talk to her?" Callahan was urgent.

"I'll talk to her," Dave said. "Now have some lunch."

"Thanks, but"—Callahan rose, looking at his watch—"I've used up my time. Have to get back to work." On his way out, people crowded around him, asking for autographs.

Watching, Leppard said, "If you don't look out, this will turn into a celebrity place. Then how will you handle the crowds?"

15

HE WOKE AT three thirty and showered, making the spray very hot in the hope of soaking out what remained of the ache in his joints. He put on worn jeans and an old cambric shirt, and crossed to the cookshack. The oven needed cleaning. He tied on a long red wraparound apron, and was squatting to get spray can, sponges, latex gloves from under the sink, when knuckles rattled the screen door. He stood up, squinting. He couldn't make out whose shadow was cast by the westering sun on the screen.

"Samuels." The pale detective came in. "We got word while Leppard was at lunch. Deputies in Contra Costa County saw a man stealing license plates off a pickup truck on a country road at five this morning. Guess who he was."

"Len Gruber," Dave said.

"He and Tessa are on their way from the airport now. The lieutenant figured you might like to come downtown."

"Stealing license plates?"

"To put on his Toyota to throw the police forces of eleven western states and Canada into confusion."

"The gun," Dave said. "Did he have the gun?"

"They didn't find one—not on him, not hidden in the car, not in their luggage. He says he never had a gun, so how could he throw it away? They questioned Tessa separately—no conflict."

"Zach didn't see any gun." Glumly Dave shed the apron, laid it over a chair back. "I asked him at Madge Dunstan's."

"Don't feel bad," Samuels said. "We'll zap Len for beating Zach up. And Tessa for not reporting him. And both of them for stranding their child on the coast road."

"I sure as hell hope so." A blue lightweight windbreaker hung by the door. He took it down and shrugged into it. "What about Klein?"

"There's nothing to hold him on," Samuels said. "Until we have brother Herschel's revolver, we won't know whether it was the one used on Shales, either, will we? While he was with Leppard at the department, I took a team and went over his place, house, garage, yard. We didn't find any gun."

They left the cookshack. Dave pulled the door shut. They headed for the road. "I'd say Klein probably had the best motive of anybody in this case. Shales had corrupted his only child, ruined her life, alienated her from her family." Samuels opened the door of an unmarked city car for Dave, and he eased himself stiffly into the seat. "The man hated Shales, and here was a chance to get back at him. His attitude these days is that his life is over. Maybe he figured he had nothing to lose." Samuels got behind the steering wheel and slammed the door.

Dave asked, "Did your team find a flight jacket in his closet?"

"I didn't ask them," Samuels said.

"Ask them," Dave said. "Just for me."

Len Gruber didn't look cocky anymore. He looked seedy and hopeless in his orange jailhouse jumpsuit. And as sore at fate as a man his age could look. A public defender sat beside him in the interrogation room, Ruben Goetz, a plump young man in a cheap gray lightweight suit. He had rigged fasteners for his attaché case from Velcro—someone had broken the brass latches. Leppard stood against the interrogation room wall again, in shirtsleeves again, arms folded across his sturdy chest again.

"You went out looking for Zach this last time," he said. "When he crept out to try to find Toyland School by himself. Why didn't you go looking for him the night of the shooting?"

"I told you," Gruber said, "I was asleep, zonked."

"That's what you said," Leppard agreed, "but maybe you were mistaken. Maybe you remembered it wrong. Maybe there was a commercial break in the TV show you were watching, and you got up to go to the bathroom, and you looked into his room and he wasn't in his bed. Tessa would chew you out when she got home from work and he wasn't there—so you went looking for him. What time did this happen?"

"It never happened," Gruber said. He looked at Goetz. "Do I have to answer this garbage?"

Goetz said to Leppard, "He doesn't have to answer."

"Damn it, Rube, I need witnesses to the Shales shooting," Leppard told him. "I've got next to nothing to go on there. I need somebody who got a good look at the shooter." He took hold of the chair back where his jacket hung, leaned over the chair, put his face close to Gruber's, and shouted, "What time did you go out looking for Zach that night?"

Gruber sat and sulked. Finally he looked up. "If I tell you what happened that night, what will it get me?"

"It won't get you off for beating your child," Leppard said. "We don't plea-bargain child abuse."

Dave cleared his throat. Leppard stepped to him, bent over him, listened while Dave whispered in his ear. Leppard frowned to himself for a minute, stroking the white streak in his hair, then nodded, straightened, turned back to Gruber. "We could probably do something for Tessa," he said. "Jail is no place for a beautiful woman like Tessa."

"What about Zach?" Gruber said.

"What about him? He'll go to foster care, someplace they know the difference between a child and a punching bag."

"Don't be intemperate, Lieutenant," Goetz said. "Nothing's been proven yet."

Leppard said, "I apologize, Counselor." He looked at the sullen Gruber again. "The county likes children to be with their own parents if possible," he said. "As Mr. Goetz says, nothing's been proven against you, yet. Maybe Zach had another one of his famous accidents. Maybe he got out of the car at that filling station to play hide-and-seek with you, and you didn't miss him till you'd driven all the way to Contra Costa County." Leppard smiled. Dave was glad the smile was not directed at him. Leppard said, "Maybe the judge will send you and Tessa and Zach to Disneyland for a week, all expenses paid, as a model young American family." Then his vein of humor ran out. He became a menace again, bent into Gruber's face again, and asked, "Now tell me about the man who shot Cricket Shales."

"I didn't go out to look for Zach. Like I told you, I was in bed asleep. The gunshots woke me up. That was when I went out. We ain't right over it, but some way our bedroom gets the noise from the swimming pool—late parties, drunks, diving board banging, splashes in the water. Pain in the ass. I was sure these shots come from that direction. And I headed that way, and down the stairs. And I seen this guy crouching down in the pool. It's empty, you know."

"I know."

"In the corner, at the deep end, like he was hiding. I heard somebody running away." He peered up at Leppard. "Must have been that Ruby Fine, right?"

"Rachel Klein," Goetz said.

"With your little son," Leppard said.

"I didn't hear him," Gruber protested.

"He was barefoot," Dave said.

Leppard said, "Forget that for now. What about the man in the pool? Did he have a gun?"

"Yeah, he had a gun." Gruber barked a laugh. "Damn right. He seen me, too. I ducked back up the stairs before he could blow me away. You better believe it."

"Describe him," Leppard said.

"White guy, around my age"—Gruber moved his shoulders, wrinkled his brow—"what can I tell you? He looked like anybody. The light was bad. They don't maintain the ground lights around that complex worth shit. He was down in the shadows. And I only seen him for a split second. Soon as he heard me and turned to look, I cut out."

"What was he wearing?" Leppard said.

"One of them leather flight jackets," Gruber said. For a moment his eyes went dreamy. "Damn, I sure would like to own one of those. But they cost a bundle." He focused on Leppard again. "You going to get Tessa off? She didn't do nothing wrong. Hell, she cried when I said we couldn't look for Zach at that filling station, we had to get out of there. She cried and bitched at me for miles to turn back and find fucking Zach. I finally had to hit her to shut her up."

Goetz winced. "Don't say things like that."

"What did I say?" Gruber asked him blankly.

Supper was chicken Marsala and asparagus tips. Dave set the plates on the table, switched on the television set, and sat down across from Cecil, who was smiling over his plate and tucking a red napkin in at his collar. "Super," he said, and then looked at the television screen because Dot Yamada, the Channel Three news anchor, spoke his name. "And now here is Cecil Harris in an exclusive interview with renowned Los Angeles drug counselor Jordan Vickers." And there were Cecil and Vickers seated facing each other behind the news desk.

"Jesus Christ," Dave said.

The on-screen Cecil was talking about the murder of pop guitarist, drug dealer, ex-convict Cricket Shales—the photo shown was a blurry snapshot—sketching in the background quickly. The real Cecil held his fork poised over his plate and looked at Dave surprised. "What's the matter?"

The on-screen Cecil said, "At his famous rehabilitation center for drug addicts, Tomorrow House"—file film of Tomorrow House—"Jordan Vickers was instrumental in the recovery of Cricket Shales's onetime girlfriend Rachel Klein, whom Shales had introduced to drugs." Footage of Rachel Klein with arresting officers. "Ms. Klein was for a time held by police for Shales's murder, but those charges have now been dropped, in part as a result of Mr. Vickers's testimony." He turned from looking into the camera to ask Vickers, "Can you tell us what it was you told the police?"

The camera pulled back for a two-shot. Vickers was self-possessed, serious. "That I received a telephone tip on the night of the murder that Cricket Shales might be attempting to contact Rachel Klein at her apartment. I wanted to prevent that if I could."

"And when you got to the apartment, what happened?"

"I saw two men fighting in the patio."

"Two men?" Cecil said. "And then what happened?"

"There were gunshots." Vickers gave a wry smile. "I made myself scarce after that."

"But you can say that it was not Rachel Klein who killed Cricket Shales, but some man. You told me earlier that he was in his thirties. Were you able to identify him?"

"It was too dark," Vickers said. "It was midnight."

"Suppose you saw him again?" Cecil said.

Vickers shrugged. "I might recognize him."

Dave jumped up and switched off the television set. He stared at Cecil, unbelieving. "How could you?"

"What do you mean? Councilman Hernandez brought him to the studio. Said you'd cleared it when he talked to you at the house."

"Cleared—?" Dave laughed. "You didn't believe him."

"He seemed surprised you hadn't told me."

"I'm surprised he knew who you were," Dave said. "He didn't give me a hint."

"Me either," Cecil said. "I'd have said he thought I was the houseboy. Anyway"—he smiled apologetically—"to tell you the truth, I didn't see how you had any right to clear anything. So after Hernandez left, I put Vickers in a dressing room with a cup of coffee and a doughnut, and I called Leppard. And he said Vickers is under suspicion, but there's no evidence to hold him. I checked with the district attorney's office, and they haven't even heard this part of Vickers's testimony. They certainly haven't muzzled him. So Vickers is free to say whatever he wants. Right?"

"Right." Dave nodded wearily, picked up his napkin, unfolded it deliberately, laid it in his lap.

Cecil said, "See, I do know my job."

"And you did your job." Dave picked up his fork. "The public has a right to know—yes?"

"It wasn't in the *Times*," Cecil said.

Dave tasted his supper. "He didn't go to the *Times*."

Cecil peered at him, frowning. "You saying they wouldn't have printed it?" He laid down his fork. "What? Hernandez sized me up as a stupid kid?"

Dave twitched him a smile. "I think you can expect a handsome present soon."

Cecil sat straight, offended. "He didn't offer—"

"A bribe? No, of course not," Dave said. "But a man like Hernandez scrupulously rewards those who help him."

Cecil looked stunned. "He used me?"

Dave nodded. "I'm afraid he did."

"Shit!" Cecil jumped up from his chair so it banged the wall. Tears filled his eyes. "Shit, shit, shit! When am I ever going to stop being a fool?"

"The same time as the rest of us," Dave said. "When they drop you into the ground. Sit down. What he did to you is nothing to what he's done to his friend Vickers."

Cecil didn't sit. "What do you mean?"

"Until you put him on the air," Dave said, "only Leppard and I knew he'd seen the man who killed Cricket. He came so close to the two of them fighting in that breezeway, he almost bumped into them. Why didn't the killer see him? He's not easy to miss. He couldn't chase him down then because Rachel was coming, wasn't she? And the killer had to hide, himself. But now—now the killer has seen Vickers again, hasn't he, knows his name and where to find him."

Cecil licked dry lips. "You mean I set Vickers up to be murdered?"

"No more than Vickers did, himself," Dave said. "He must have sensed after that interview with Leppard that he was a suspect for murder, and it worried him. So he called Hernandez for help—what else are powerful friends for? And he played right into Hernandez's hands. The councilman advised him to clear himself of the murder charge by taking his story to the court of public opinion. Hernandez would arrange for it himself. He knew someone at Channel Three news who would help him out."

"Oh, Lord." Cecil moaned, and looked at the ceiling.

Dave went on, "By telling the viewers of the six o'clock news he saw the killing and the killer, Vickers would change himself from a suspect into a mere witness—or so Hernandez claimed." Dave took another bite of chicken, while Cecil watched him, agonized. "He suckered Vickers first. Then he suckered you."

"Why?" Cecil cried this, bewildered, frantic. "Why?"

"Because Vickers knows a dirty Hernandez family secret," Dave said. "And in Hernandez's very shrewd judgment, Vickers cracks under the slightest pressure, and the pressure of a murder investigation is in no way slight, not when it focuses on you, and it was beginning to do that to Vickers, wasn't it? Vickers betrayed Rachel to save his own hide. And she meant a lot more to him than Alejandro Hernandez. If he thought it would help him, wouldn't Vickers just as easily spill what he learned the night of the murder when Hernandez rang him for help?"

Cecil reached up for the phone, and held it out to Dave. "Get Leppard to give him police protection."

"I'll try," Dave said, and took the phone.

Lying on the couch in the rear building, reading the new mystery Jack Helmers had handed him the other morning, Dave heard the coachwork of Amanda's red Alfa-Romeo squeak as it zipped down into the yard from Horseshoe Canyon trail. It was a familiar sound and a welcome one. She'd had the car it seemed forever. He hoped she'd never get a new one. It had become in his mind such an extension of herself. He marked his place in Jack's book with the jacket flap, laid the book under the lamp, laid his reading glasses on top of it, and got up. He was already on his way to the door when her footsteps sounded in the courtyard. He could tell from the click of her heels she was in a testy mood. He opened the door.

"Right on time," he said. "Come in. A drink?"

"Dave, I wish you wouldn't—" She broke that off, gave him a tight little smile, a quick little peck on the cheek. "Oh, yes, of course, a drink, and then"—she plumped down in one of the red leather wing chairs—"a long, Dutch avuncular lecture to straighten me out."

"You've been peeking at the script." He lifted a hand in the doorway, and after a moment the ground lights in the courtyard went out. He smiled and closed the door. He walked up the room, past his desk and file cabinets, to the dimly lit bar. "Cecil's out. Brandy?"

"And soda, please." She wore off-white jeans, a big floppy boy's cap, oatmeal color, a bulky oatmeal color sweater, a yards-long muffler. The size of the chair made her look tinier than ever, but red was a color that favored her prettiness, though it needed no favors.

"It's a shame to treat brandy like that," he said.

"Europe does it," she said, "and I'm over there so often now, it's come to seem natural." He fixed brandy and soda for her, no ice, and got himself brandy neat in a small bubble glass, and came back to her with these things, gave her what she'd asked for, and sat down on the couch again with his drink.

"He's a nice straightforward kid," Dave said. "Forget the others. Don't pile their faults on him."

"We had an understanding." Amanda sipped the brandy and soda. "No show-biz shenanigans. Not for me."

Dave lit a cigarette. "He doesn't like them either."

"Oh, Dave, he's bought into them," she said impatiently. "They come with the territory. Actors sign contracts. They don't control what they do or what's done to them. I knew that. I don't know why I didn't remember it earlier."

"Because Cliff's different from the rest of them," Dave said with a smile, lifting his glass to her. "And you knew that from the start."

"I was in love and I believed what I wanted to believe."

"He didn't do this to you, Amanda."

"Hah!" She tucked up her feet. "Then who did, pray?"

Dave heard muffled sounds outside, and glanced at the door. "I invited you here tonight to meet him."

She narrowed her eyes. "Him?"

Dave shrugged. "Him, her. We'll see in a minute."

Amanda stood up. "What are you babbling about?"

"I never babble." Dave got up and went to the door. "Cecil will introduce us." He pulled the door open.

And through the doorway, propelled by a shove from behind, stumbled a youth, whining and cursing in Italian. His black hair stood up spiky. He was so slight his trendy wide-shoulder jacket looked borrowed. Two cameras hung around his neck. A bulky photo equipment bag bumped his hip. Behind him, Cecil came in, grinning.

"Wasn't any time at all," he said, "when I heard him crackling around in the bushes."

"Who are you?" the youth demanded of Dave. "What do you mean by this—this—assault? I will call the *guardi*. I will tell them—"

Dave put a hand over his mouth. "Listen a minute. You've been following this woman, haven't you?" He nodded to indicate Amanda, who stood by the fireplace watching in bewilderment. "Well, I will tell that to the *guardi*, and the *guardi* won't like it. You mustn't do that."

The youth knocked Dave's hand away. "I am photographer." He was panting. He rummaged in the bag. "Here, see? My press credentials." He waved a creased paper at Dave.

"Good for you. But harassment isn't covered by this."

"I'm-a no harass," the youth said, glaring at Amanda. "She is VIP. Newsworthy. The public—"

"Has a right to know?" Cecil looked irony at Dave and went along the room to get himself a drink. "Forget it."

Dave said, "You've been taking her picture for days now. Isn't that so?"

The boy nodded. "Yes. Why do you object?" He threw Amanda an impudent grin. "She 'as no object."

"She didn't know," Dave said. "I knew."

The boy looked him up and down. "You? I 'ave never seen you before, 'oo are you?"

"I'm the lady's relative," Dave said. "And I knew you existed without having to see you. Somebody was telling the studio that makes "Icarus" all about the lady and Cliff Callahan. It was you, wasn't it?"

The youth shrugged. "I am professional photographer. They buy my pictures. It is 'ow I live."

"And one of those pictures showed the lady and Cliff Callahan at the Hall of Records downtown, isn't that right?"

"You are charlatan," the youth scoffed.

"You are wrong. I'm a real magician," Dave said. "Else how did I know you'd turn up here tonight? How did I know to have my friend ready to catch you?"

"This is craziness." The youth turned and reached for the door. Dave stepped in front of him.

"Just one more minute. Tell me if you took such a picture. What harm can it do?"

The youth eyed him narrowly. "If it can do no 'arm, why are you so excite' about it?"

Cecil came back. "Because it can do some good," he said. "There's been a misunderstanding between the young lady and her fiancé. You don't want to wreck their love story, do you? I thought Italians were romantic."

The boy sneered. "You tap dance, I play mandolin." Cecil raised a fist in mock threat and grinned.

The youth grinned back. "Sure, I take that picture."

"And went inside and showed the clerk your press card and asked if the lady and Mr. Callahan had taken out a marriage license, right?"

He shrugged. "I already knew they take blood test."

Amanda gasped. "What? But doctors' records—"

"Are sacred?" Dave said, and looked at the youth. "Is nothing sacred?"

"Nothing you can buy for twenty dollars," the boy said, snatched open the door, and fled into the night.

He left them laughing for a long time.

16

POLICE PATROL CARS stood at angles in the street, doors hanging open, lights revolving on their tops, pointless in the early morning sunlight. Dave left the Jaguar at the curb down the street and jogged toward the shingled turrets of Tomorrow House. A black-and-white and an unmarked police car stood in the driveway. Radios crackled from the cars, static jolts interrupted by the voices of female dispatchers. Only two officers were there to hear. Uniformed. They stood by one of the cars, talking, a black, an Asian. Dave showed them his license. Nice-looking kids. Dave wondered when they'd left high school—last week?

He told them, "Lieutenant Leppard sent for me."

They peered at the license. The black one said, "That's right. Go on in, Mr. Brandstetter."

The front door stood open, but the gap-toothed girl in coveralls was nowhere to be seen. Nor was anyone else. The television in the big room to the right of the hall played cartoons but no one was there to watch. The metal folding chairs in the other room were empty. A uniform looked at Dave from the end of the hallway beside the staircase. Dave showed him his license and said his piece again, and was waved on. He had a feeling he'd end up on the back porch, and he ended up on the back porch. It was milling with men, but the center of attraction lay dead under a linty brown bullet-punctured blanket on his monkish cot. Jordan Vickers. He was having his picture taken. Cameras flashed.

Leppard appeared beside Dave. "I want you to look at it." He pushed men aside, taking Dave to the body.

"He was reaching for the phone," Dave said.

"Looks like it," Leppard said.

Dave stood looking at bed, body, bedside table, lamp, telephone, clock radio, screened window above the bed. Vickers's thrift-shop clothes lay over a chair, wallet, loose change, keys. Dave crouched and peered under the bed. Big shoes. The cap with BOSS on it. He pushed painfully to his feet, dug out his reading glasses, bent close to the blanket. It smelled of that same cologne he'd breathed the other morning in the interrogation room. He studied the blanket, straightened, tucked the glasses into his jacket pocket.

"Shot at close range," he said to Leppard, "by what I'd guess was a thirty-two."

"Three shots, just like Shales," Leppard said.

"Only this time, he used a pillow for a silencer," Dave said. He looked around him. "Anybody find that pillow?"

"No sign of it," Leppard said. "Some more of that lint outside. He must have taken it with him."

Dave moved between men to the outside door. The screen had been cut, a hand thrust in to work the hook. "For a man with so many chancy acquaintances, he put up a poor defense."

"Door says it wasn't one of the inmates," Leppard said.

"Door to the hallway locked, was it?"

"No. They tell me never."

Dave gave his head a marveling shake. He glanced toward the desk and files. "Nothing there?"

"Fingerprints will tell us. I doubt it. He came for only one thing—to kill the man that saw him shoot Shales."

Dave grunted. "One of them. When did it happen?"

"The ME will tell us."

Leppard nodded at a bony man with gray skin, a slack mouth, long teeth—Carlyle, who shambled to the bed with his kit, giving Dave a sour smile as he passed. He hated being kept waiting. He glanced around him as if he couldn't quite believe his turn had come. Then he uncovered the long lean body on the cot. Jordan had slept naked. Dave turned away.

"Nobody heard the shots?"

Leppard led the way into the hall. "Nobody will admit they heard the shots, heard anybody prowling around, heard squat. And maybe they didn't, but they're not types who like talking to the police. They're types who figure whatever they say, they'll end up in trouble."

"Where are they?" Dave said, and walked into the empty rap session room. "The place is usually teeming."

"They were all packing to leave," Leppard said. "I ordered them to stay." He glanced up the stairs. "In their rooms, I hope." A uniformed officer appeared at the top of the stairs. Another high school type. This one blond and blue-eyed. Leppard called, "Everybody still here?"

"Detective Samuels isn't through talking to them yet," the blond boy said. "They're all still here. But they don't like it. They don't call me by my right name."

Dave lit a cigarette. "What's his line of questioning?"

"He's after gossip." Leppard held out his hand. "You have one of those you can spare?"

Dave's eyebrows went up. "You, Lieutenant?"

"Never mind that," Leppard said, took the pack from Dave's hand, got a cigarette from it, set it in his mouth. "This is a crazy case with no end to it." Dave lit the cigarette for him. "He's trying to find out if anybody was sore at Vickers. Nursing a grudge. Whatever."

"We know who did this," Dave told him.

Leppard blew smoke away and snorted. "Plain Vanilla?"

=Dave said, "Plain Vanilla."

"Businesslike bastard." Leppard flicked ashes into the empty fireplace. "Gruber's lucky to be in jail."

"But Rachel Klein is out of jail," Dave said. "I hate to give unwanted advice again—"

"Here it comes," Leppard said bitterly. "'I told you so.' You warned me to protect Vickers and I brushed you off. Never again. I've already sent people to watch out for her."

"She back at her apartment?" Dave said.

"You want to tell your TV buddy? You think that will draw the killer, and my men can bust him when he shows up?"

Dave shrugged. "He sure as hell watches the news."

"Plain Vanilla." Shaking his head in disgust, Leppard moved into the hall. "'Looks like anybody,' Gruber said."

Dave followed him. "Well, we know now that Vickers saw Shales's killer, all right, poor bastard. So did Gruber. And it wasn't Rachel, it wasn't Karen Goddard, it wasn't Irwin Klein. Who does that leave?"

"A drug dealer," Leppard said. "Who works the area around that apartment complex. The first idea is sometimes the best, right?"

Dave said, "Tessa Gruber said drug-related shootings were common around there. Have you checked them out? Maybe this isn't Plain Vanilla's first."

"Hell, yes, we checked them out." Leppard glared at Dave and tossed his cigarette off the porch into a flower bed. "No loose ends in any of those."

"Loose ends enough in this one," Dave said. "Which reminds me—there's something I forgot to do."

"What's that?" Leppard said.

"Look at Cricket Shales's personal effects."

"Help yourself," Leppard said. "There's nothing there."

A uniformed officer, this one no kid, a veteran with a beer belly, on the verge of retirement, looked at Dave through the black-wire mesh of the property department with eyes that had seen too much of the wrong kind of life. Dave remembered him but not well. Siekmeier was the name on the plastic-enclosed identification tag on his shirt pocket. He said, "Brandstetter, isn't it? Been a long time."

Dave smiled a little. "I hear that a lot, lately."

Siekmeier chuckled. "Yeah, me, too." With a wince and a soft groan he slid his weight off a stool. "What can I do you for?"

"Shales," Dave said, "Howard Ronald, also known as Cricket. Homicide victim. His worldly goods?"

"Yeah." Siekmeier went to a steel mesh gate, rattled keys, swung the gate open. "Come in." Dave did that, and Siekmeier closed the gate again and led him down aisles of green steel shelving piled with cardboard cartons. He peered left and right as he went, then grunted, stopped, hauled down a carton. He nodded. "Table down there."

"Thank you." Dave carried the carton to the table that was also of green steel. He set it down and pulled up the flaps. Wristwatch, wallet, jeans, jockey shorts, T-shirts, a cheap fleece-lined jacket, tennis shoes. Music paper, much of it written on. Well-worn paperback books, all of them about pop singers, jazz artists, rock groups. A meager sheaf of letters. He took a rubber band off this, put on his reading glasses, sat on a stool to scan the letters. Five were from Rachel Klein. Eight were signed Alan. Rachel's were pleas for forgiveness and preachments against drugs. Alan's were mostly happy memories of the music business. Dave wished Shales had kept the envelopes. It would be nice to know Alan's last name and his address on Easy Street. Cricket had evidently put him there, and he was grateful. Anything he could do for Cricket when he got out of prison, all Cricket had to do was ask.

When Dave unfolded the last letter, a snapshot fell out and fluttered to the floor. He laid down the letter, got off the stool, bent painfully and retrieved the snapshot. He sat on the stool and studied it, frowning. It showed three slim young men, long-haired, one with an electric guitar, one with a Fender bass, one boxed in by keyboards. They were grouped on an outdoor stage cluttered with microphones. Part of a banner in the background had gotten into the photograph. It said ESTIVAL. The guitarist must be Cricket. The bass player was dark, with sunglasses, something feminine about him. The keyboard man had stood up, smiling, and raised his right hand in a wave. He wore a beard. Dave turned the photo over. *Alan Marsh, Brice Tyner, Cricket Shales. August 1985.* What might be a town name came next, but the ink had gotten wet and it was unreadable. So were three words in a sentence that ended *forget this? Wasn't it the greatest?*

Dave looked along the aisle. Siekmeier sat on his stool at the counter, his broad back turned. Dave slipped the photo into his jacket pocket, loaded the carton again, and returned it to the shelf from which Siekmeier had taken it down. He went along to the gate. "Thanks, Siekmeier," he said. "Leppard said there was nothing there, but one man's nothing can be another man's something. I had to look."

"Anytime." Siekmeier got off his stool again and opened the gate so Dave could go out. "Be seeing you."

"Of course," Dave said. "We're always bumping into each other, aren't we?"

"Like clockwork," Siekmeier said. "Every twenty years."

The woman at the musicians' union in Hollywood had flame-colored hair and lipstick and immense flame-colored frames to her glasses, but she had no record of any Alan Marsh in her computer file. No, he hadn't transferred to another city or state—there'd be a record of that. Musicians travel all the time. The locals had to have records of everybody. No—plainly Alan Marsh had dropped out of the music business.

"It happens. Lots of them fall by the wayside after a while. You can love music, but a person has to eat."

Cricket Shales's name was still on the rolls. He had evidently paid his dues, San Quentin or no San Quentin.

"You can take him off, now," Dave said.

"Oh—why is that?"

"He died," Dave said. "Just a few days ago."

"I'm sorry to hear it." She used flame-colored fingernails to nip a dead nasturtium from the arrangement on her desk. "The birthdate on his membership card makes him only thirty. What happened—AIDS?"

"It could have been," Dave said. "He used needles. But it wasn't. It was murder." She gave a gasp and her eyes opened wide.

Dave said, "The police have run out of leads. Marsh and a bassist called Brice Tyner used to play with him. I hoped they might give me an idea of who would want him dead."

"Really?" She picked up and studied Dave's business card again. "Well, I can't give you Brice Tyner's address, but there's no rule against your seeing his agent." She rattled fingers on her keyboard, studied the screen, scribbled on a note pad, tore off the slip, handed it to Dave. Above her note it read *From the desk of Renata Schwartz*, and beneath, HAVE A NICE DAY. "That's the address," she said.

"Thank you," Dave said. The hike down hallways from her office seemed long, and as he pushed out of the building into noon sunlight, he was suddenly dead-tired again.

Ninety minutes later, numb with fatigue, he dragged himself up the outside stairs of a Sunset Boulevard motel and came dishearteningly close to shuffling to the unit number he'd been given. He knocked. He knocked. He knocked again. At last, the scuffed red door jerked open, and a naked young man squinted at him. His long dark hair was tangled from sleep and he was pawing strands of it from across his face.

"Yeah, what is it?"

"I'm Brandstetter," Dave said. "Didn't Kalish tell you I was coming?" Kalish was the agent, a man with frizzled red hair and too many clients, too many telephones. He worked in an enormous Beverly Hills agency, and Dave had napped in a leather armchair in his handsome vestibule for an hour waiting to get to see him. "He said he'd phone ahead."

Brice Tyner nodded and backed into the room. "He phoned ahead. That didn't mean I don't have to sleep, did it?" He wasn't self-conscious about his nakedness. Why should he be? His body was perfect as a Greek marble. It reminded Dave of Kovaks's body long ago. "Come in," Tyner said. He found a muslin shirt on the carpet, picked it up, flapped into it. Its tails were almost knee-length. He didn't trouble to button it. He sprawled on a couch. "What's this about? Ol' Cricket?"

"He won't get any older," Dave said. "Somebody shot him to death the other night." A television set was in the room. Dave glanced at it. "It was on the news."

"I missed it." Tyner yawned. "Anyway, last I heard he was in jail."

"You never wrote to him there," Dave said.

"Listen, we weren't buddies." Tyner jumped up and went away for a moment. Dave heard a hard stream of urine crash into a toilet. The toilet flushed. Tyner came back with a Diet Pepsi and plumped down on the couch again. "We had a trio for a while, five, six years ago. "A and B and the Cricket." It never went anywhere. We broke up." He shrugged. "Nobody cried. It was strictly a business deal. We used to see each other at recording sessions sometimes. Cricket just for the hell of it made some arrangements for the three of us. We gave it a try."

"Alan Marsh did write to him in jail," Dave said.

"That right?" Tyner blinked at Dave over his soda can. He appeared surprised. "Well, you never know."

"Never know what?" Dave wondered.

"I thought they were both straight," Tyner said. "I'm the gay one."

Dave smiled thinly. "I'd never have guessed."

Tyler smiled back, stretched, and the shirt fell open. "I was hoping you would."

Dave said, "I'm flattered." Dear God—the child was Kovaks more than just in body. "But my sleeping partner wouldn't like it. At the musicians' union, they told me Marsh has dropped out. Where is he, do you know?"

Lazily, watching Dave with his mind on something else, Tyner scratched his lean belly. "I ran into him once—someplace, last year, year before?" He stood up, came and stood in front of Dave, the shirt open, his hands on his narrow hips, grinning. His penis stirred and swelled. "Bedroom's just in there," he said. "The sheets are clean."

Dave stood up quickly. "Where was it you saw Marsh?"

"Some store." Tyner dreamily caressed himself. "The Gap? Miller's Outpost? Clothes, okay?"

"Did he say how he's making his living?" Dave said.

"He said"—Tyner smiled—"'Why work when you don't have to?' Cricket had introduced him to somebody with lots of money who needed help around the house—something like that." Tyner leaned forward and put a kiss on Dave's mouth. It tasted of the heavily sweetened drink. He tried to take Dave's hand. "Come on. I'm lonesome. 'The Lonesomest Girl in Town.' You ever hear that? Some old singer called Kay Starr. You ever live in motel rooms? It's the pits."

"I know," Dave said. "How did Marsh look?"

"Different," Tyner said. "No more long hair. No more beard."

"Thanks. Keep well." Dave put a light kiss on his mouth, and left.

When he reached Horseshoe Canyon trail, he drove past his own place up to Hilda Vosper's, a brown cottage tucked in among trees, on the downhill side of the road. He turned in, so the Jaguar nosed her garage doors, and climbed wearily out. Hilda Vosper had a little raggedy brown dog. Now on the other side of the front door, the dog barked in bright, nonstop excitement. There was no need to press the bell button. After a moment Hilda's cheery voice called that she was coming. And soon the door opened. Wiggling happily, the little dog sniffed Dave's shoes and pants cuffs, gave him a bark, and bustled away on some errand of his own.

"Dave!" his little owner cried. "How nice! Come in."

"I've come for a favor," Dave warned her.

"Anytime, you know that." Her very blue eyes blinked at him, concerned. "You don't look well."

"I'm a little tired," he admitted.

"Come outside with me," she said, walking brisk as a girl across a comfortable living room, and out French doors to a rear deck set among treetops. It was a beautiful spot. Years ago, when Cecil was recovering from gunshot wounds, he'd spend a lot of time down here, in the calm and quiet, getting his strength back. There was a good smell of pine and eucalyptus in the air. Today, Hilda had set up an easel, a work stand, and a canvas director's chair for herself. There was a second chair of the same kind. She motioned Dave to it. "Sit down. I'll get us some tea in a minute."

"Don't go to any trouble," Dave said.

"The water's heating," she said. "Just let me try something here to see if it works." She picked up a brush, dabbed it in a mound of paint on the tabletop, and tilting her head touched up a clump of greenery on the canvas. It wasn't a picture of her backyard she was painting. She was working from a photo attached to the easel above the canvas. Somebody's house by the ocean, and far down the beach two people riding horses. "I feel these days if I stop working, I'll keel over and never be heard from again."

"I know the feeling," Dave laughed.

She stepped back to study what she'd done to the green. "Yes," she told herself, "that was what it needed." And she laid the brush down, and turned to look at him. "Now— satisfy my curiosity. What favor can I possibly do you?"

"You've done several." Dave laughed.

She smiled. "I couldn't have my favorite neighbor kidnapped by thugs in the middle of the night—now could I?"

He took the snapshot from his pocket and held it out. "You showed it to me once—a projector you've got that blows up photos so you can trace them on canvas."

She took the picture and studied it. "Yes, I remember. It was new then, and I was so pleased with it."

"Is it still working?" he wondered.

"Oh, yes. You want a painting of these boys?"

He pushed to his feet, stood by her, put a finger on the picture in her hand. "That one in particular."

"The one with the beard?" She gave him a smiling nod, took the picture away with her into the house. "Let me get the tea." Dave sat down and was asleep when she returned with the tray and set it on a squatty rough redwood table among potted plants. "You are tired, poor man," she said, seating herself and pouring from a wicker-handled blue-and-white pot into matching cups, cups without handles. She handed him one. "I brought cookies. You look as if you could use a cookie. You're too thin."

"Thank you." The cup was hot. He set it on the table and bit into the cookie. "It doesn't have to be a painting. I don't want to put you to that trouble. Just a drawing will be fine." The cookie did taste good. She was right. He was hungry. He ate it in two bites and reached for another. "But I'm going to impose on you to make two."

"Ah, well, I can use my copying machine," she said. "It's wonderful the machines we artists have these days to help us out. When I was a girl I never imagined it all."

"I don't mean two the same," Dave said. "I mean two different. Please."

Her eyebrows rose. "Different? How?"

"On one," Dave said, "give him a shave and a haircut."

17

WYNN-MADDEN REAL ESTATE was up a small side street off Sunset Boulevard in the heart of Hollywood. Or it had been. The name was still on the window, but the glass was dirty and rain-spotted. A CLOSED sign hung on a string inside the glass door. The sign was fly-specked. Beyond it stood desks with nothing on them but dust. The floor was strewn with papers and glossy black-and-white photographs of houses, photographs that were turning yellow. In a corner three white telephones waited on the floor, their cords wrapped around them. A red-and-white pasteboard FOR RENT sign sagged against the window. The word OWNER and a telephone number had been lettered on it in black marker pen. It was fading away. Dave found a pay telephone on Selma Street and called the number. He learned what he expected to learn, and went back to the Jaguar.

Chaim Chernov wore pajamas and a robe this morning, and on his hairless skull rested a black-and-red smoking cap. Its silk panels had long lost their gloss, and the tassel was moth-eaten. From his wheelchair in the doorway, he blinked at Dave against the bright sunlight. The Santa

Ana winds had blown again in the night and scoured the sky. The day was dazzling. "Who is it?" he asked.

"Dave Brandstetter," Dave said.

"Ah, the man who found Rachel. Did you know? She is no longer suspected of murder. I have paid her bail, and she is, for the present, a free woman."

"Yes, I know," Dave said. "That's good news."

"A great relief," Chernov said. "Such a magnificent voice. The world needs music, Mr. Brandstetter."

"I agree," Dave said. "Is Arthur here?"

"He is at the supermarket." Chernov backed his chair. "I expect him soon. Come in."

"Thank you." Dave stepped inside and shut the door. The broad living room with its handsome furniture, carpets, paintings, was chilly. Chernov was studying him with his blurred old eyes. Dave asked, "What is it, Maestro?"

"I—I was just wondering if—" But he didn't finish. He shut the question down. He seemed embarrassed.

"Is there something I can do for you?" Dave asked.

"Well—I—have a little mystery," Chernov said, and laughed at himself. "It's nothing, really. But you are a skilled investigator. Yes." He nodded, and the smoking cap slipped, and he reached up to settle it with a trembling hand. "Let me show you." The wheelchair hummed off down the room. "Come with me."

Dave followed him. "A mystery? You mean there's been a crime?"

Chernov laughed. "Has there, hasn't there? Who can say?" He stopped the chair in the dining room. "Things go missing, Mr. Brandstetter, and then they reappear as if they had been here all along. What kind of thievery is that?"

"Which things?" Dave said.

"On that wall"—Chernov pointed—"hangs a small Manet landscape, a watercolor sketch."

Not now. Now a flower painting hung there. Vuillard, by the look of it. Dave stepped around the long table and lifted the picture down. It was the same size as the dark rectangle around which the wall's paint had faded slightly.

He hung the flowers back, turned, and searched the old singer's ravaged face. "Are you certain, Maestro?"

"You think I am losing my wits?"

"Everyone makes mistakes," Dave said.

"The Manet has always hung in that spot."

"What about the Vuillard?"

"In the second bedroom," Chernov said.

Dave got his directions, found the second bedroom, looked around, called back, "There's an empty space for a picture in here."

"Just so," Chernov said. "What does it mean?" Dave went back to him, shaking his head.

"You see?" Chernov exulted. "Isn't that a mystery?" He lost his smile. "Or do you think as Arthur does—that it's the medication addling my wits? I tell you, things disappear, and then they're back again. You'll see. Tomorrow or the day after, the Manet will be in its rightful place again. It's happened over and over."

"Yes, I expect it has." Dave glanced around. "Anything else besides the paintings?"

"Ah, you see, how well the trained professional mind works. Yes, indeed." He made a gesture at a sideboard where an elaborate silver service shone. "Those—all of them—vanished one day, and were back the next."

"I believe it." Dave smiled at him. "But it's not much of a mystery."

Chernov's eyes opened in surprise. "You have solved it—so soon?"

Dave nodded. "I have information you don't have. That made it easy. It's my reason for being here this morning—to share this information with you. It will take a little time. Are you comfortable here? You want to go back into the living room? Or perhaps you'd like to lie down."

The old musician shook his head impatiently. "No, I'm all right. I'm bored to death with lying down."

Dave drew out a chair and sat at the polished table. He laid on the table the big white envelope Hilda Vosper had fastened with a pushpin to his door early that morning, before he and Cecil were awake. "First I have something to show you," and he opened the envelope and slid out a drawing. He put it in Chernov's hands. The old man's dim eyes peered at it, and he smiled.

"Why, it's Arthur," he said. "And very nice work, too." He squinted, looking for a signature. "Who is the artist?"

"A neighbor of mine," Dave said. "Hilda Vosper."

"I don't understand. Is this a gift for me?"

"I don't think you'll want to keep it," Dave said.

Chernov frowned. "What do you mean? Why not? This young man has become a son to me, Mr. Brandstetter. My life would have ended long ago if it weren't for Arthur Madden."

"The young man in that picture is named Alan Marsh."

Chernov looked blank. "What are you saying?"

Dave took the snapshot from the envelope. "Can you see this clearly? Examine it, please." The old singer glanced at the windows, turned his chair so the light from the windows fell on the smiling images of A and B and the Cricket on that sunny outdoor stage, and held the photograph close to his eyes for a time. Dave said nothing. He waited. At last Chaim Chernov sighed, lowered the snapshot, and gazed at Dave with tears in his eyes. "Why did he tell me he had no gift for music?"

"He told me that, too. It's part of his new identity. The real estate broker. Wynn-Madden is out of business, Maestro. The real Arthur Madden died year before last."

"The real—?" Chernov was pathetic in his bewilderment. "But, but—he came here because he had heard I was ill and wanted to put this building up for sale. He brought papers for me to sign. Imprinted Wynn-Madden."

"You didn't sign them, I hope," Dave said.

"Not those, no, but I have signed many papers for Arthur. He is my heir, I have no one else. He has looked after me with great care, tended to my every need, he—"

"He's an impostor, Maestro," Dave said. The snapshot lay on the table. "Did you see who else is in that photo?"

Chernov gave a sick, sorry little nod. "Cricket."

"That's right. They were friends. Arthur didn't come here by accident. After Rachel brought Cricket here to meet you that time, Cricket told him about you and your illness and all the beautiful priceless things in this apartment. He was struggling to stay alive in the music business. He hated struggling. He wanted to be rich."

"But—I pay him nothing," Chernov said.

"He manages your finances, doesn't he? Writes the checks, banks your income—rents, dividends, royalties?"

Chernov looked down at his hands, clasped in his lap. "Such things are beyond me, now."

"Then he can help himself to whatever he needs," Dave said. "Isn't that so? You trust him completely."

Chernov's head remained bowed. "Completely," he whispered. Then, with a brief flare of indignation, he glared at Dave. "He has never betrayed my trust."

"I hope not," Dave said. He slid the pictures back into the envelope, and stood up. "But he's been taking your paintings out to be appraised at auction houses. That explains why they've been disappearing and reappearing. He's greedy. He wants to know how much you're leaving behind, Maestro, when you die—down to the last penny."

The sick man was terribly white. He didn't speak. He simply stared miserably into Dave's face.

"Where is his room?" Dave asked.

"It is the servant's room, back of the kitchen," Chaim Chernov said. "I tried to dissuade him. He might have had either extra bedroom. But no. He insisted."

Dave figured he insisted because it was up two little steps—wheelchair proof. It was cold and anonymous, like its occupant. There wasn't even a picture on the wall. He opened a closet. There among clean shirts, slacks, jackets, sweats, a business suit, hung the flight jacket. Shoes lay on the floor, loafers, brogues, Nikes. He picked up the Nikes. Stuck to the soles were long pine needles, brown, like those fallen into the empty swimming pool near Rachel Klein's apartment. Crumpled in a corner of the closet lay a black sweater and jeans. He smiled. They were snowy with lint. He opened drawers. Underwear, socks, sweaters, and under them a .32 Colt revolver. He stared down at this for a minute, then left it where it was. He didn't need more, but he suspected there was more, and he went into a small bathroom. On open shelves lay folded towels, washcloths, bath mats, on a wash basin a toothbrush, toothpaste, a throwaway razor. Cans of shave cream, deodorant, and hair spray stood side by side. The door of the medicine chest was a clean mirror clamped in chrome. He pulled it open. On glass shelves inside lay small clear plastic packets of crack, a glass pipe, and a Bic lighter. A voice said:

"What the hell do you think you're doing?"

Dave closed the cabinet and looked at Alan Marsh in the mirror. Hilda Vosper had gotten him just right. He had the gun from the drawer in his hand. Dave said to him, "It's too late, Alan. You should have stuck to your keyboards."

"You've got the Maestro very upset," Marsh said.

"Better upset than dead," Dave said.

"What do you mean?"

Dave said, "The man pointing his gun at your back will explain it to you. I'm tired of explaining." The man was Jeff Leppard. Behind him, Joey Samuels held handcuffs. "You got my message," Dave told them. "That's nice."

It turned into a long day. He had a kind of grudging affection for Parker Center, the jangling telephones, the rattling keyboards, flickering, beeping terminals, the constant movement of cops in and out, the wails of sirens on the streets below, prisoners, witnesses, lawyers coming and going, arguments, laughter, emotions running high and low like fevers. But by the time he felt free to leave today, he'd grown weary of it. Maybe even nauseated by it. He climbed aching into the Jaguar and put the new tall glass towers of LA at his back gratefully, heading out the freeway for Laurel Canyon and home. He hauled himself up to the loft, rid himself of his clothes, laid his aching bones on the bed. He didn't look at the clock. He didn't care how late in the day it was. If Cecil came home and found the way he slept scary, it couldn't be helped. He had to rest. He woke at some point in the night when the bed moved. Cecil sat on the far side, pulling a shirt off over his head.

"Hello," Dave said to his lean glossy back.

"So it was this Alan Marsh, was it? Plain Vanilla?"

"I told you on the phone," Dave said.

Cecil lay beside him, propped on an arm, looking down in the starlit darkness. "All about the flight jacket, the shoes, the lint, and how Len Gruber identified him."

"I also told you about the gun."

"The lab tests weren't in yet."

Dave turned onto his side, and his eyes fell shut. "It was the same gun that killed Cricket. No question."

"Mr. Klein's gun? And Marsh took it from him?"

Dave sighed and murmured, "Marsh picked Cricket up at the airport in the maestro's car, drove him to his parole officer, then to a cheap motel. Cricket said he'd pick up some crack and they could meet that evening and smoke it. Marsh went, and Cricket told him the plan he'd thought up in prison—to kill Chaim Chernov and make it look like a break-in and robbery."

"Don't tell me, let me guess," Cecil said. "Cricket would do the killing while Marsh was out someplace public, establishing an alibi—and afterward, they'd split Chernov's estate between them."

"The paintings alone are worth millions."

"So what went wrong?" Cecil said.

"Marsh claims he was revolted by the plan," Dave said drowsily. "He loves the maestro. My God, did he give him two years of tender loving care just to end up killing him?"

"But the truth is, he didn't want to split the profits with Cricket, right?"

"You've grown cynical living with me," Dave mumbled. "I'll never forgive myself for that."

"But all the same, Marsh drove Cricket to Rachel's to pick up the gun he planned to use to kill Chernov, and Marsh waited outside, fretting. When, as luck and Karen Goddard would have it, along came little Mr. Klein with his gun. And Marsh jumped him from behind, took it from him, and shot Cricket when he came out of Rachel's place?"

Dave was drifting. "Marsh was infirm of purpose, and Cricket almost got away from him."

"His purpose firmed up later," Cecil said glumly.

"Worse luck for Jordan Vickers," Dave said, and fell asleep.

He woke early. His stomach did it to him. He hadn't put anything in it since breakfast time yesterday. He crept out of bed in the gray dawn light, picked up clothes, and went softly down to the bathroom to shower, shave, and dress. Then he crossed to the cookshack to start coffee and heat some croissants as quickly as he could. He was taking butter out of the icebox when the phone rang. He didn't want it to waken Cecil, so he ran for it. The sudden haste made his heart hammer. He grabbed the receiver. The voice at the other end belonged to Jack Helmers.

"Dave? I've been robbed. Can you get up here?"

Dave groaned. "Call the police, Jack."

"I don't want strangers. I want you."

Helmers said, "Look at the mess he made." He'd brought Dave through the living room that looked forlornly empty without its heaps of newspapers, magazines, junk mail, junk in general, to the door of his workroom. Inside, green words glowed on the computer monitor in a corner by a window, the cursor light blinking. But the stacks of manuscripts and magazines and books and clippings were all over the place. "Threw stuff around like a maniac."

"Too bad," Dave said. "I'd recommended this room for the Good Housekeeping Seal of Approval."

"Not funny," Helmers said. He wore another cotton flannel shirt. This one had been washed and the dryer had shrunk it. It had popped a button over his big belly and showed a gap of T-shirt underneath. "I'm working," he complained. "I can't afford these interruptions."

"What time was this?"

"Don't know. Asleep upstairs. Didn't hear a thing."

"What about the dogs?" Dave stepped into the room.

"Wish I knew. They're not watchdogs, they love everybody. Been driving all over the neighborhood, calling them. No luck. That worries me more than what he stole."

Dave crouched and began picking up stacks of pages. His heart began to labor. "Which was?"

"Can't you guess? The Pasadena novel, the big one. And I mean, he took everything, disks, notes, drafts, and four copies of the final manuscript."

"And nothing else?" Winded, Dave straightened with his paper burden and looked around for a place to set it down.

Helmers took it from him, gave it a glance, grunted, and perched it on top of a storage cabinet. "That was it."

"But doesn't your agent have copies?" Dave said.

Helmers shook his head. "I got sore when everybody kept batting it back." He scowled to himself. "Never been so humiliated. Been writing novels for twenty-five years. Now, suddenly, I don't know how."

"Jack, your new book's getting great reviews."

"The mystery," Helmers snorted. "I can write those in my sleep. This book meant something, God damn it."

"They all mean something," Dave said. "Stop feeling sorry for yourself."

"Oh, I have. But it took a while." He left the room, making for the kitchen. "And at the time, I got on the phone and called in every copy from wherever it was, New York, London, Tokyo, all over. The way everybody was sneering at it, I didn't want a trace of that book left anyplace on earth. I wanted to bury it. Come on, coffee's ready."

"You overreacted." Dave's jaw began to ache. That was novel. What did it mean? Probably nothing. He went along. The kitchen looked dismal without its empty cans, frozen-dinner trays, bottles—stripped, soiled, lifeless. But the smell of brewing coffee was welcoming. He found butter and English muffins in the grubby refrigerator. "It wasn't you. You said it." Now he began hurting between his shoulder blades. "The book publishing business is changing."

"It's the damn buyouts." Helmers filled mugs with coffee. "Nobody cares about the product anymore. They fire everyone who's built the business, and put in kids with milk on their chins to run things, and"—he thumped the mugs on the unwashed table—"suddenly writers like me are nobody. If you can't please half a million readers, forget it."

An ache started in Dave's left arm. He rubbed the arm while he watched the toaster. It was old and scorched and he didn't trust it. He kept flipping the lever to check on the muffins. After three checks, they were nicely tanned, and he laid pats of butter on them to melt. He found a lone salad plate in a cupboard, wiped the dust off, put the muffins on it, and set it on the table. "Jam?"

"Probably all moldy. Honey be all right?" Helmers fetched a tin bucket from the icebox, clunked it on the table, thumbed off its lid. "Neighbor used to bring us a couple of these every year. Best honey I ever tasted." He spooned some on his muffin, bit into it, chewed. "Place look better to you cleaned out? Goodman's coming in to paint it next weekend." He took another bite, and went on with his mouth full. "Good kid. He's offered me a deal, too, and I'm taking him up on it. He buys the house now, lets me live in it rent-free till I die, then it's his."

"Don't trust him," Dave said.

Dogs began a commotion outside, barking, scratching at the screen door. "Great God," Helmers said, jumping up, bumbling out of the room. "Duffy, Molly, is that you?"

Dave followed him to the front door. A limousine was sliding out of the driveway. Helmers banged out through the screen door and crouched, hugging and crooning to the dogs, who licked his face and whined. "Where have you been?"

"Dognapped," Dave said. "And see what else has been returned." A carton stood at the foot of the stairs. He fetched it, climbed back with it, legs weak, short of breath, set it on the rail and pulled open the flaps. Floppy disks. Manuscripts. "Could this be your Pasadena book?"

"You're kidding." Helmers struggled to his feet, the dogs still jumping around him, excited, happy. He peered into the carton. "By God, it is." He shielded his eyes against the sun and looked down the driveway. "Did you see who brought it?"

"I saw the car," Dave said. "Morse Campbell's."

"I hoped it was," Helmers said. "Dumb bastard." He laughed. "All that worry, all that trouble, having me watched, trying to bribe me, finally resorting to breaking and entering"—he wiped away tears of mirth from his stubbly face—"and all for nothing."

Dave stared at him. "For nothing?"

Helmers clapped Dave's shoulder, grinning. "There isn't a word about him in it—there's not a word about any of you."

"But you let me think—"

"Mostly, it's about me and my father."

"Hell," Dave said, "I wanted to be immortal."

"Sorry about that," Helmers said, "but once I heard how worried everyone was, I had to go on with the joke. I meant to go on with it till the book was published—if it ever is."

"It livened things up." Dave rubbed his aching arm.

"I'm just sorry I couldn't see Morse's pop-eyed face when he read it." Chuckling, wagging his head, Helmers picked up the carton and carried it back into his sad house, Duffy and Molly jumping joyfully around him.

Dave turned to follow, and pain laid a red-hot iron bar across his chest. He grabbed for the deck rail. "Jack," he said. It came out faint. He tried again. "Jack?" Then he wasn't standing anymore. He was on hands and knees.

Helmers appeared in the doorway. "Jesus, what is it?"

"Paramedics." Helmers turned to run a heavy old man's run for the phone. And Dave was on his face on the deck. "Don't trust Goodman," he whispered, and then he couldn't breathe, and the pain was fierce, and it was morning, so it wasn't supposed to be dark, but it was dark as night.

Joseph Hansen (1923–2004) was the author of more than twenty-five novels, including the twelve groundbreaking Dave Brandstetter mystery novels. The winner of the 1992 Lifetime Achievement Award from the Private Eye Writers of America, Hansen was also the author of *A Smile in his Lifetime, Living Upstairs, Job's Year,* and *Bohannon's Country.* He was a two-time Lambda Literary Award-winner.